Her name is Dra—. That's D, heroine of Stacey Levine's first r story about a woman whose ide. make almost no moves toward adult life is both haunting and laugh-out-loud funny.

The novel turns that most banal of activities, the search for a job, into a nightmarish pilgrimage of regression and lost selfhood . . . In polite, literate prose that evokes Kafka, Levine characterizes the quest for employment as a virtually hopeless bid for access to some kind of normalcy. The demands of the adult world seem arbitrary if not malevolent, and Dra— is repeatedly derailed in her job search by her longings to succumb to passivity and infantilism. A visit to an employment agency provokes in her an overpowering—and hilarious—craving to go to the doctor, to lie down and be examined for an internal disorder, or even more attractive, to be in the presence of the doctor's bewitchingly understanding Nurse.

Dra—'s dreams of being cared for like a child are regularly denounced by other characters, who seem to have x-ray vision into each others' psyches. At one point, an employment manager says to Dra—: "You're afraid of others' feelings, aren't you? You'd do anything to avoid anger, even stop defecating, wouldn't you?"

As this suggests, the novel takes place at the site of the earliest human issues. Levine even uses overtly Freudian underpinnings, at one point having Dra— nestle jealously between a man and a woman who are trying to have sex . . . [But] Dra—'s sexuality is located at such a submerged area of childish fantasy that it could scarcely be termed a "drive." Levine evokes the early stages of longing with beautiful, arresting prose:

> Once, Nanny had carried Dra—'s heavy books through the hallway with one bluish, straining arm... Nanny had lifted the books easily and with great calm, a gesture that had caused Dra— to flood inside with an unendurable sweetness so close to illness that she in fact sat sickened all that day, bent, limbs apart, daydreaming fitfully of Nanny's high, stark forehead and thinly vibrating voice.

Adult sexuality is a faraway land from the psychic territory of this novel, which seems to be a pre-Oedipal swamp of fear and dread. In the modernist tradition yet in a voice that's entirely her own, Levine puts the emotional violence of human relations under a high-power microscope, producing a memorably funny narrative that is hauntingly unusual.

—Kristy Eldredge, *Third Coast*

ALSO BY STACEY LEVINE

The Girl with Brown Fur
Frances Johnson
My Horse and Other Stories

Dra—

Stacey Levine

VERSE CHORUS PRESS

Published by Verse Chorus Press
PO Box 14806, Portland OR 97293. www.versechorus.com

First published in 1997 by Sun & Moon Press

Book design by Transgraphic (www.transgraphic.net)
Cover photograph: *FIF #4 (K)* by Robert Stivers

ISBN 978-1-891241-31-4 (paper)
ISBN 978-1-891241-83-3 (ebook)

Library of Congress Control Number: 2011926398

WHEN SHE LOOKED at the man sitting at his work desk, she noticed that most of his hair was gone, not as if it had been shaven, but as if it had fallen out, perhaps recently. Dark and light patches of scalp showed through, along with all the veins, knots, and other unsettling irregularities of his head.

She had never actually spoken to him, the slight, thoughtful-seeming man, though he had been there for many months in the same set of dim workrooms as she; he had been in the auditorium, too, during the first moments she and he and dozens of others had become eligible for employment. She also had seen him during the three days she had spent traveling to the low, remote set of offices where the fact of this eligibility had been confirmed, and she remembered him hazily from the distant past as well. And now, momentarily, he was before her again, sitting motionlessly behind stacks of paperwork as she made her way past a series of narrow hallways with their gruelingly close workrooms.

She did not know the man's name, although she had seen him many times; so in her mind she began to refer to him as The Man with No Hair, despite the fact that he had hair, though not much.

And overall she did not think of the man very often at all, because she had been so absorbed lately with finding a job, a very important task—so important, in fact, that she, like everyone else, needed to follow through with it unerringly and never fail.

But it was really only a matter of searching for good, solid work until something turned up. Naturally she would check telephone messages at every reasonable moment, and search the endless lists of jobs posted in the hallways, too—lists which always rotated, since new positions were cropping up at various times throughout any given day; and even as the map on the wall before her now indicated, jobs were constantly shifting in their availability, and were in fact virtually limitless in number, so that really, it was only a simple matter of matching oneself to the right job, seizing the opportunity, then fiercely beating back all thoughts of disgrace.

But at any given moment, she, Dra—, knew that droves of would-be employees were searching for jobs, flooding the message centers entirely of their own wills with flat, anxious voices that no one heard, wishing out loud just for a chance at a reasonable, attractive job, or any tolerable job at all—yet it was impossible to know if she would ever find one, or if anyone ever would or had. But it remained that all employee hopefuls were competing at every moment for work—she knew this with sightless certainty, in the way one senses the puzzling presence of one's own being—such that very few jobs were ever available, and it was next to impossible to find one.

Walking on, purse clamped tightly beneath her arm, it seemed the image of the man slipped from her mind because she could not hold it there, and she told herself not to worry about jobs, since worry was damaging to the heart, brain, kidneys, and stomach; and didn't employees sometimes die from ailments whose sole cause was worry? It was best not to worry, since finding an attractive job was more important than worry any day—yet, she thought suddenly, now stepping up her pace, why hurry so? What was the point in hurrying to find a job, since surely one must come, in time? But she had been wasting days and even weeks, she answered herself, and should have found a job long ago, and should be finding one now. It would be much healthier to find a job slowly and with dignity, then calmly hold onto it for decades—that was much preferable to worrying wrenchingly over never finding a job and then being consumed by all the worries and shame that joblessness always brings.

But finding work was a near-certainty. Her very first job would be just one of many, many jobs she would hold throughout her lifetime, she knew—all jobs being the same, of course, yet all of them quite different, too—the nature of any single job being to sweeten and change subtly over time. Still, no one could ever really define the true, exact nature of any given job, even if one held it for decades, because jobs were, in their essences, evolving things, and always mysterious.

On the other hand, one could become quite knowledgeable about all the countless jobs that existed, too, their finer points and subtler demands—and the ways they might be grouped and regrouped according to the

8

admixture of their duties, their titles or lead administrators, or even by their humorous aspects, though only a veteran of decades would be able to classify them that way; and really, she wondered, much struck, mightn't it be impossible for any one person, even an administrator, to know every detail about every job? Yes, that would be a task for an entire organization, she realized, still walking carefully along—the Employment Office, of course—and it was toward this office that she now walked.

And in these dim empty hallways with their lingering odor of toilets and chalk, memories scaled colorlessly through her mind as she pressed on. She recalled walking down a narrow, endless hallway years ago—it might have been this very hallway, though that was impossible to know—and seeing her own doctor, a man, reclining in a womanish manner against a cabinet, wearing, possibly for warmth, a shawl, quietly intoning to someone, perhaps another doctor, "It was only a small swelling on his forehead; I did nothing more than push it, just to see what it was, that's all. And do you know, the next day that boy died?" And puzzling, uncomfortable over this recollection, she also remembered the time, years before that, when she had stood silently beside the school fountain— a poor excuse for a fountain, really, since it had consisted only of a pitiful stream of ink dripping into a makeshift pan, and since the fountain, also known as "The Song," was always broken in numerous, complicated ways detailed on a nearby plaque—how on that day, she gagged after catching a bit of the fountain's warm, fetid odor, which perhaps was the smell of the school itself, with its clamoring, upset students, long mottoes, and teachers grown so furious that they vanished; and that day, she began, for no reason that she could discern, to spit into the fountain again and again with a vehemence which puzzled her, until a guard shambled over to her, leaning his hands on his knees, cocking his head and remarking to another guard, "Look at that anger, will you?" then leading her away to the cool apartment of rooms where the principal lived.

But now, continuing to walk through these long hallways, she shook off such memories, smoothing the length of her iron-colored skirt, concentrating instead upon the Employment Office, where she was now headed, with its enormous waiting area and rows of backless chairs nailed to the floor in sprawling semicircles, and upon her upcoming interview with the Manager there, and how she must, despite all defeating odds, procure a job.

She would have to settle on what type of job she wanted, of course, and articulate this clearly to the Employment Manager. But that would be easy; it was easy to think about jobs, of course: what was really difficult was to think about anything else.

But the most trying thing would be to restrain herself in front of the Employment Manager and not to behave cloyingly just because a job might be close at hand, or just because she would be sitting close to the Manager, necessarily an important, exciting woman; but instead, head level, to hold out for the right job, the best job, or at the very least, a simple, solid, generous job, a straightforward one, upward-facing and flexible: for all in all, that would be the way to a broader life and overall release.

But she must not expect the perfect job right away, she

cautioned herself then, quickening her step; instead, she should merely focus on finding a job, any job, nothing more, because a perfect job, one that fit the employee's needs and character in every way, was not something to expect now, but far in the future, one of the pleasures of older age and long experience.

And so she walked, feeling something nearly like hope inside her, and thrust out her chest sharply once, as if waiting for self-possession to arrive and fill out her flesh, though when it did not, she sighed. She recalled a letter she had received a few months before, scribbled on a thin gray length of stationery that for some time had been stuffed into the bottom of her purse, a letter which had welcomed her to the ranks of job-seekers—she recently had come of age—yet strangely, the letter had been written by an official of enormous importance, of rank so stupefyingly high—judicial, most likely—that it seemed inappropriate, though the letter only wished her the best of luck for as long a life of work as would be reasonable to expect.

The letter, she recalled, with its greasy, cramped characters, first congratulated her for her desire to be employed, also stating that, though this letter was no guarantee, she might, with time and luck, land a good job, nothing promised, but that a decade hence she would surely look back at this frustrating period with a smile, at that point being deeply acquainted with the satisfactions of steady employment; so right now, she should not worry, for worry was a destroyer. Besides, there were plenty of employees with far worse problems than she, the letter explained; for instance, those with diseases so disturbing, so out of the realm of the imagination, that they could not be described in a short letter; and she should not think about disease in any case, the letter remarked, because, though it was not a certainty, a fulfilling job might soon arrive for her, like a fantasy, overnight.

So the letter had been kind, she had thought at first, but later, considering it further, she began to see that the letter was rather blithe and suspicious too; and now, moving onward, looking back over the past weeks in deep retrospect, a hunted feeling scudding through her stomach, she saw how cruel the letter actually had been: for it promised nothing and counted for nothing, in terms of leading to a real job. Besides, it attempted to conceal the fact that finding such a job was as uncertain as would be the manner of her death; and in a way, she felt the letter tried to prefigure her entire existence as nothing but a series of spiraling downfalls and general embarrassments.

Yet she had been unable to discard the letter, instead saving it fondly for some time in her purse, deriving pleasure from the fact that she had received a piece of correspondence at all. Over those weeks she imagined, with enjoyment, that the letter had not been cruel, but instead wonderful, overflowing with rollicking news and repartee, that it had made an outright guarantee of full-time work, and also that its writer was a stern authority to whom, she especially liked to imagine, she was quite close.

But beyond sinking into these imaginings, there was nothing else to do right now except continue to look hard, hard as anyone who looked diligently for a job in this world, because jobs brought with them a new stage of life; it was a good job that everyone most hoped for, in any event, since jobs brought relief, allowing an individual to shine as never before.

So with pride she realized that she had many important things to do—finding a job being one of them, but also, protocol demanded she write a thank-you note to the author of the letter.

For some reason, however, she was unable to bring herself to compose the reply. Instead, she carried the letter with her for weeks, the task evading her constantly, until finally one night, sleepless, chewing through the skin of her fingers, upset by the burden of the entire month during which, she realized, she had accomplished virtually nothing and had not spoken a word, she abruptly returned the letter to the sender. And the brilliance of this act struck her: it was probably the most succinct message the man had ever received in his life, and later, who knew, he might seek her out and reward her for her cleverness, she considered, and grew warm.

Returning the letter had been virtually the only act she had been able to complete lately. So it surprised her that she was actually able to move ahead with the job search, and that she was now walking, almost breezily besides, toward the Employment Office; yet, who wouldn't do the same? she considered, for there was really nothing else to do.

Moving along in this way, feeling the dull, heavy sensation in her bowels that came from the habit of holding everything back, she tried to tell herself that despite the strange feelings the letter had given her, she would eventually find a job and be settled. Some positions required oral recommendation; some required exhaustive tests: the letter could not help her in either of these areas, she thought bitterly. Letters counted for so little, in any case, often being supercilious or forged; and with a sudden sense of contracting finality, she realized how utterly, profoundly worthless the letter had been, that beyond being cruel, it was sheer mockery. It probably had been a form letter, anyway, despite its smeared, scratchy characters. It was a laughable letter, she finally decided, and perceived that in this business of looking for a job, there was nothing, ever, to grasp onto, aside from one's own spasmodic habits of striking blindly ahead—and so in this way and no other, she would simply continue to search, as shamelessly as instinct is shameless, traveling steadily and without issue, just as she was doing now, toward the Employment Office. There, she would simply beg for a job.

Closer now to that office, she entered a bright hallway, this one lined with glass cases containing various color annuals and journals, attractive pictures on their covers of employees who were now dead. At the Employment Office, she thought, growing nervous, competition would be rough, and she might be denied jobs, gems of jobs, because of deficits in her character she had failed to resolve.

But for now, she continued to walk. Despite the silence of these halls, there were, she knew, thousands upon thousands of employees everywhere, not visible now, but hard at work instead, gathered in small stifled work centers, basements, and sub-basements; night stations, corridors, and portable and permanent work areas; work vaults, niches for special projects, and training hutches connected by hallways just inches across that stuttered in one direction then another before widening into empty classrooms lined by shelves full of sheets and old surgical equipment.

Hundreds of feet down the hall, she made out a cluster of people walking toward her. Over minutes, as they drew closer, she discerned that they were new hires in training, among them an agile, thin man with an unusually thick head of hair who spoke to the group rapidly and enthusiastically. Against his chest he held something small and dark.

Folding her hands, moving to the wall, Dra— huddled, waiting for the group to approach, and furtively she stared at the gesticulating Lecturer, who, as he passed, raised the dark object over his head with his hands, calling out gaily over his shoulder, "A puppy! Last of its kind, or almost!"

Indeed it was a small animal that the Lecturer held, perhaps as some kind of instructional aide; and with avid gestures, he exclaimed variously, smacking the animal's flank, describing the ways the world tended to open and flower for those who had made firm, intelligent choices in life, adding that superior nutrition was always available to people who were already healthy. He mentioned exercise, then added how difficult it was for most people to resist gentle or even violent physical touch, and how, in the end, everyone succumbed to it.

As the group looked quietly on, the Lecturer, shifting his moist, avid eyes, discussed general rules of the workplace and the procedural errors that employees most commonly made—none of these errors really being, he explained, minor: each told significantly of the individual's conflicts and weaknesses, so they were apt starting points for deep analysis.

"This afternoon," the Lecturer went on, pulling on his stringlike tie, "I'm also going to tell you about success— that it does not exist, except in one small way, that is! All your lives, you see, you have achieved success in its basest form—by surviving. You've all survived by adapting so precisely to the environment that your identities have become lost. Identity slips away, you see."

Smirking, blinking, the Lecturer then went on to explain house rules, hoisting the limp, sleeping dog into the air again, then he gave two definitions for the word "courage."

"None of you need worry about what you call 'success' anymore," he told the group. "What does that mean, anyway? As it turns out, most everyone does well, after all. You'll have long-lasting jobs, a sense of safety, and storage space, too. Just stay alive, then you'll see! Everything will happen like clockwork. Hasn't it always been this way?" He sighed with what seemed a mixture of content and defeat.

"The threat of failure isn't quite real, you know. But there are worse things." He laughed unpleasantly. "Soon, you'll have advanced on the job more quickly than you ever dreamed. Leisure time—that is, hours of your own to sit in a straight chair—you'll have that too, when you're older." He handed the dog over to a student helper who affectlessly slipped the animal into a soft sling that hung at his side.

"Your lives will take shape before you realize it," the Lecturer said, "and what will happen after that? Nothing, except some of the people you know will die. Years will pass, ill health will set in, but by then, life will be almost over anyway, right?"

Then the Lecturer began to describe an employee perquisite system so vast and effervescent that there was no other system to compare it to, he said, laughing again, and the students laughed too. One, a young man, shook his patchily haired head and said, "What did you mean just now, about success? What you said isn't true. Success exists—look at me, I spent every day of my youth preparing for success, and now, I've got it! Nothing to sniff at, sir. How can you say success doesn't exist?"

"Pretty easily," grinned the Lecturer.

"But I am successful!" the young man, Russ, said angrily. "Look around you—all of us here have succeeded! We're young, we're bright, we've all been accepted into the hiring pool. We're doing just as we should!"

"Ah! Can you tell me more about what you think you should be doing, Russ?" the Lecturer asked gently, touching his fingertips together. "Don't censor yourself—express everything, please."

Russ reddened. "Well, it's not easy to succeed . . . but at the same time, everyone I know has done it," he said. "When we apply ourselves, life gets better, you know—instead of feeling low, we feel proud, and so does everyone around us. So why not do it? From the start, I was a good candidate for success: I work efficiently, I'm good with my hands, and besides, I'm debt-free!" He grinned, looking around, shyly pleased that he had gained an audience.

The Lecturer chuckled, tucking his chin into his hand. "What do I care what you think? Should I say, 'You're an idiot,' though you're better off than me? Should I bother? The world is going to stay the same whether you're burdened by awareness or not!"

"What are you talking about? I may be wrong," Russ cried, "but I feel you're insulting me!"

Eyes weary, the Lecturer dismissed the topic with his hand, and as Russ stared mutely and angrily after him, he led the group of trainees down the hallway, describing a political system completely invisible because ubiquitous. After this, he called out brightly, "Let's press onward! Bound for the cafeteria we are, to receive instructions on meals and the washing of both head and shoulders!"

As the group moved passively along, Dra— noticed that one of them hung back and turned to stare at her, a tiny, red-faced woman with small red eyes whose face was somehow familiar, and somehow, from a distant place in her mind, Dra— recalled that the woman's name was Nanny. Beyond all doubt, her name was Nanny, yet it was impossible for Dra— to remember how she knew this, or to remember anything else about this Nanny, who in these few moments only continued to stare steadily. Dra— lifted her hand toward Nanny in a lilting, halfhearted gesture then turned away; but unable to stop herself, she looked back once again at Nanny, who took several weak steps toward her as the Lecturer and group turned to watch.

Dra— tried again, and the effort was cinching, yet she could recall nothing about this woman besides the name, and so decided that she was probably confused, that this woman was not Nanny, but someone else—so many employees looked alike, anyway: irritated, raw-faced—

and that would be a great relief. For she did not want to know the nearsighted, unpleasant-looking woman who was now stepping closer, scowling, squinting, emitting a flat "Hello!" and a dry, cloaklike scent like rats that made Dra— recall the gruesome sensation of being close to someone with little hope for escape.

And after a long minute, Nanny took another step, sniffing, blinking, and broke into a wide, strained smile that stretched the skin of her small face painfully, and lurching forward with a small kiss of greeting, she began to kiss Dra—'s hair, and the air all around her face, too, and a chirruping sound issued from her throat; it was a high sound, and difficult to like.

A gale of dizziness arose within Dra—, and then she realized, as if with a thump to the chest, that she did know Nanny, after all; that, though it was now unimaginable, she and Nanny once had known each other well; Nanny had been her teacher, no less; and she remembered the nervous hands, the fixing watery eyes, the high noise in the throat, all of which were Nanny, only Nanny. Stunned with this realization, eyes tearing, Dra— reached forward to chastely pat Nanny's bone-thin arm while gaping all the while in amazement at her. This was the woman to whom she had clung close during unending years of school so long ago, years when the other students had raged and torn around endlessly, calling for an end to just about everything in life while shaming Nanny, who had screamed back at them in wordless despair as night melded into day again and again until finally they, the students, abandoned Nanny en masse just for the pleasure of it, knowing that she was too weak to stop them. And throughout, Dra— had stared from the back of the classroom at Nanny, who with her tiny cries had sent Dra— into a frozen dream.

Once, Nanny had carried Dra—'s heavy books through the hallways with one bluish, straining arm; she had carried them as a favor, fingers spread wide beneath the stack; though extremely small, Nanny had lifted the books easily and with great calm, a gesture that had caused Dra— to flood inside with an unendurable sweetness so close to illness that she in fact sat sickened all that day, bent, limbs apart, daydreaming fitfully of Nanny's high, stark forehead and thinly vibrating voice. Meanwhile the other students stormed through the school, their faces dark-red—the area had never been intended as a school, in fact, but rather as a furnace—screaming excitedly, involved in all sorts of intricate battles that were not games; she also remembered mornings of utter darkness when she had waited for the little teacher to arrive and unlock the door to the school room. Several times, Nanny had beckoned to her from across the classroom, and just once, Nanny had beckoned in order to reach out slowly and zip up Dra—'s uniform, for strangely, the zipper had been fully undone, with Dra—'s back and sides entirely exposed, though it was hard to imagine why. Nanny was also a mother.

And Nanny, once so robust and energetic, once bearing such full, chestnut-colored hair, was now wizened and agitated beyond recognition, almost, and also, bald, except for the pale-reddish strands that lay smoothed against her right temple like baby's hair. Fearful, gazing at Nanny, Dra— asked as suddenly as a reflex: "Are you ill?"

"Of course I'm ill," Nanny snapped, legs sticklike, apart, continuing, "partly because of you. I haven't forgotten you, and the way you conceal your thoughts! You were always horribly quiet, to the point that it was sheer manipulation! I say it's high time we talk about the feelings."

And Dra—, hand at her throat, aghast, said only, "What feelings?" to which the Lecturer standing a few feet away gave a great horse laugh, and the rest of the students laughed as well.

Ashamed, not knowing which feelings Nanny meant, while vaguely suspecting the dreadful worst, which itself she did not quite know, Dra— stood disbelievingly in silence.

Nanny burst forth, waving one hand, "You, just being who you are, were always horrible for my health! Do you know you might have killed me back then? Why should I submit to that? I'm the sort who gets everything off her chest and holds nothing back—did you know that about me? When I need to air my feelings, I do so, and if you can't do it too, then that's your misery, lady. Until you are able to do it, you aren't a whole person and even past the age of thirty-five you're still considered a baby unless you can talk like a grown-up!" Nanny gasped for breath.

"This is all quite nice," the Lecturer broke in, "but we don't have time for such talk—I have a training to give!"

"Unreleased feelings are agony, and agony is hell," Nanny blustered on, addressing everyone; "haven't I paid enough to learn that? Oh, don't pretend; we all know because we're educated, just like any other piece of educated charnel! The world is ugly and distorted till the moment we release our rage—and we all have rage, my dear!" She rolled her eyes broadly, clutching her hands together, then pointed to Dra—. "I know all about you and your problems. You never could take even the smallest bit of criticism."

"But I was just a schoolgirl then," Dra— protested.

"Exactly!" Nanny cried; "that's the point—you've been this way all your life, from then until now! Wandering around like the victim of the whole world, trying to get sympathy, your woes written all across your face like a silly equation! Listen: you've got to take responsibility for your feelings and air them!"

Mutely, Dra— sought the Lecturer's face.

"Just put embarrassment aside and speak,'" he said to her. "Perhaps she's right. Besides, you see that she is an extremely sick woman; let her have her way. Of course, how many employees are just as sick as she, or even a tiny bit sicker? Scads! But then again, look at her closely—she may actually be somewhat sicker than they are."

Exhaling fearfully, Dra— asked, "What kind of sickness do you mean?"

"What the hell kind of sickness do you think I mean?" the Lecturer sneered. He looked around, considering, then addressed the group: "Most of you already know that this disease is an inevitable part of life's biology. More philosophically, you might just say that we all must suffer and die."

Russ, the student, called out, "That's not true! I don't think we have to suffer."

"Oh? Why not, Russ?"

"Well, I learned about the problem of suffering when

I was a young man," Russ answered slowly, breathlessly, a faint whistle in his speech. "Only a certain category of people suffers badly. For the rest of us, life can be fairly easy. But people like you just try to make it hard!"

Nanny groaned, attempting to speak.

"Let me finish," said Russ. "All suffering will vanish, I know it will, if we just, you know—believe in bigger things!"

"Russ, Russ," the Lecturer said. "Believing is only in the mind! Think outside the mind—think about the world. Then you might understand."

"What?" cried Russ. "What do you mean, 'Outside the mind?' I will not go outside the mind!" His eyes teared.

"You are being a little baby," the Lecturer said. "The world is just too big for you to grasp. Relax, won't you? Don't think about it. When you begin your job, you're going to feel much better all around," he grinned.

"I'm leaving! If this is job training, I'll eat my shoes."

"It is job training," the Lecturer smiled; "and I think it's interesting, Russ, that you say life is easy, yet you aren't willing to stay here with us when you find things get a bit unpleasant!" He chuckled. "Oh, never mind, Russ. Come here." He stretched out an arm. "Come with me." He said softly, "I actually know some questions that are much more important than anything you're talking about, Russ, though the answer to each of them is 'No.' Can we be close to others whenever we like? When we don't like what other people are doing to us, can we really make them stop? And when we feel uncomfortable, are we actually able to recognize it?"

"Quiet!" Nanny cried. "That is not what we are discussing! I've got only one thing on my mind, and it's this girl: she needs to come forth and express herself. I am amazed that you don't see that! Haven't I done the same? It's about time we heard about the feelings . . ."

"Oh, shit on the feelings!" cried the Lecturer. "We don't have time; or we do, but we're not matched well to the time we have. Tonight, we'll all be exhausted, dammit, and we still have to catch the late train!" He shut his eyes and placed his fingers at his temples for a moment. "Now that all this nonsense has arisen, I must address it," he said, stepping in front of the group, smoothing his hair, and Dra—, worried, dared not look at anyone but him. He spread his hands slowly and looked at the group assembled before him in the hallway, saying, "It's true that the feelings are uppermost in Nanny's mind—but that's only because her illness is worsening and time may be short. Let me go back and speak about the illness for a moment now, since it will come to you all someday. If," he said, eyes scanning the quiet group, "you look at this woman closely, you'll be able to discern which stage of the disease she's in, one, two, three, four, all the way up to ten! Can you? I can, just by looking at her." He turned to Dra—. "At least talk with her, why don't you? You wouldn't want to be responsible for making her spirits fall. Keep her spirits high, why don't you," the Lecturer said, turning back to the group, "because inner attitude may affect the body—the news always says so, though we'll never really know if it's true or not. Personally, I don't think a person's spirits really affect their health— doesn't death take us all the same, no matter what mood we're in?" He stepped back and looked at Dra—. "Oh, come along, just tell Nanny what she wants to hear!"

Nanny, seeming not to listen, railed on, "We'll get the feelings out of her, I know it. Do you think I'm the only one who's going to be vulnerable? Don't you see there's something wrong with her? The way she lives . . . it's just sick-making! Why isn't she hard at work, analyzing herself and trying to change? Well, let me tell you a little secret, Missy. If you run away from feelings, they will only come back later and kill you with their truth."

"The truth is always somewhere," mused the Lecturer.

"Can we sit down?" asked another woman, Buzzy, eyes rolling, bored, hand pressed to her face.

Dra— cried out to Nanny, "I can't talk about those things now—the whole group is listening!"

"Exactly!" Nanny yelled. "I had to speak about my feelings to a group—and so should you, every Wednesday!"

Anxious, at a loss, Dra— scanned the hallway, seeing that its length prohibited a quick escape, and as Nanny angrily reached out with a diminutive hand, perhaps trying to grasp Dra—'s shoulder, the Lecturer remarked, "When does contact become attack?" and ushered the class through a small doorway behind them.

They all shuffled through a short stone passageway in silence, until Nanny cried past the others toward Dra—, "Can't you see I'm trying to help you? Stay with me, and let me show you I get excited sometimes and then I yell and condemn because I have such keen senses, you know, but that's my lot, to have keen senses; come, stay with me a while, won't you? I hardly speak to a soul, these days!

Don't they say that speaking is a lost art? Well, it is for me. Did you know that about your old teacher? That she is all alone and much too defensive even to look a stranger in the eye or strike up a bland conversation on a train?"

"No," answered Dra— flatly over the others' heads as they moved along.

"Tell me about you," Nanny called out to her. "Who are you, these days? What about your feelings? Once, you had feelings for me."

"I don't remember!" she cried.

"Liar!" Nanny yelled. "God, why don't things come easy for me? What do I have in the world, at my age? What was I doing when I was younger, wasting all my time? And now, I don't have time!" Her voice quavered.

"Be quiet, Nanny," the Lecturer said sharply, striding ahead of the group. "Why is life always so unbearable for you? Do you think perhaps we should examine that issue before you die?"

"I only want to have what I once had! I want to smash the present, I want to go back to the past," Nanny cried. "And I want you to acknowledge that that is a natural, human need."

Dra— moved away from the group, softly passing through a small doorway to her left. Hearing the Lecturer's angry reply fading behind her, she considered that Nanny's behavior was to be expected, after all, because, as the Lecturer had put it, Nanny was not a well woman.

Nanny called out for her, but Dra— already had made headway through a low, tunnel-like hallway, only once glancing back through the doorway at Nanny, who was lurching around weakly, yelling in a thin, failing voice as the group stared stonily behind her, "Look there, she's leaving her old teacher, just like that—and why? There's no reason for it. Look, she leaves. Don't!" she cried. "When you're older, you'll want all the fondness in the world, and eye-contact too—you won't be able to have it, either, believe me, not unless you can accept it right now from someone who knows you better than anyone else in the world and if you wait too long to accept contact, you'll be ruined! Why, even now, your face is ruined by tiny eye-wrinkles, and the rest will be ruined soon, believe me!"

But Dra— was now stealing away in wide strides, powered by the momentary strength of nervousness; and as the sound of Nanny's voice faded, she noted, as if from far within herself, how easy it had been to walk away, though usually she was not able to do so.

Presently, as she walked, a terrible, meandering ache arose in her back, so she found a stair landing and sat on its cold cement to rest, shunting from her mind all thoughts of Nanny, the training group, and the entire previous hour as best she could.

She turned a keen attention to the back-pain: it seemed familiar. The sensation was often vague, and it moved; the pain was perhaps best described as a shadow, and it sometimes took on the shape of a spider, with spokes of sensation expanding from a center. It was a worrisome pain, and one, she realized, that demanded she see a doctor right away.

Rising wearily, she headed into a hallway perpendicular to the previous one, shakily telling herself that she must do two things: never again think of Nanny, and find a doctor. This last was especially important, and it would take only a few minutes of her time. Doctors, she knew, could eliminate even the most mysterious and sudden of pains, and so she hurried to find a telephone.

Naturally she would call Doctor Jack Billy, she thought, walking more confidently now; who else would it be but Dr. Billy? She had known him all her life, though for some reason it was impossible to recall his face right now. She had no memory of meeting him, either—instead, it seemed she had known him gradually and always, the absent-minded doctor of long silences and sudden grimaces, the one who breathed seriously through his nose, puffing; though long retired, he still saw patients. In the distant past, there had been a period of time when Dra— thought of him to the exclusion of everything else, and she still carried with her a photo of the two of them together, he and she, taken after a routine exam. As it happened, Dr. Billy possessed the unusual power of being able to put himself exactly into another person's position, to the point that, if only for a few moments, he could become nearly the same as anyone he wanted. In this way, he was able to speak as if he were any number of absent colleagues, and give second or third opinions; and with his easy smile and long, colorless hair, he could really resemble anyone at all, so frequently he gave fourth and fifth opinions as well.

Smiling now with these thoughts, she began to run through the hall, enthused, looking out avidly for a telephone so she could phone him, despite the lateness of the hour; and she recalled his trait of laughing mirthfully for long moments with no clear reason, then abruptly growing sour. She thought also of Dr. Billy's rather large stable of patients, a virtually endless list that expanded and contracted variously over the years while remaining steadily huge, a list full of people she would never know—and suddenly she felt ripe, agonizing jealousy rush into her chest and she yelled out sharply once, imagining herself falling hard on the tile floor again and again.

A low, wide adjacent hallway caught her eye. Looking in, she saw at its center a long bank of telephones available for employees to use; opposite, behind opaque glass doors, stood the Employment Office itself. Breathing, eager, she ran to the phones, choosing one—which was difficult and took time, since all the phones looked the same—and dialed Dr. Billy's number, an old, old number from a different era, and she wondered how such an outmoded, lengthy sequence of digits could actually create a connection. But it did; she heard the broken buzzing tones in the earpiece and decided that, if she could not be connected immediately to the doctor's bedroom, she would leave several urgent messages with the receptionist. Trying with difficulty to recall the doctor's kindish, looming face, she also decided to ask him, for once, just how many patients he really had, and if most of them paled in comparison to her, which she suspected they did. And with great relish, she imagined scheduling an appointment with the doctor, and also a prefatory appointment with his nurses—the latter in order to spend time chatting and catching up so she might quickly become involved with the office and all its workings.

The prospect of all this was so heartening that her ribs seemed to quiver. She did not want to wait for these things to transpire, but instead wished to soar mindlessly, as if upon a vapor, into the doctor's dusty little set of rooms, where she would fall upon his exam table and lie still, steadying herself against the squall of curious impulses that always rose within her while the doctor examined her, trying to determine what was wrong.

Blinking, eyes casting up and down the hall, listening to the receiver's continual ringing tones, she imagined the doctor's glowing reassurance that she was, in fact, his most important patient, the one whom, privately, he most celebrated; and smiling, she imagined asking him some questions about his own oft-repeated bodily functions, just so she could know some detail, any detail, about him. But, she imagined, the doctor, at that juncture, would become so violently angry that he would, in effect, disappear—so she abruptly hung up the phone, staring at the faint electric glow around the stall, vaguely seeking its source.

And then she realized, taking small steps away from the telephones, that she did not really want to see Dr. Billy at all; naturally she did not want to see him, but instead the Nurse, the Employee Nurse whose job it was to care for employees everywhere. And now she knew that every thought and wish she had was suddenly flowing toward the Nurse. It was naturally the Nurse she needed, not the doctor, for the doctor knew nothing of Dra—, in the end; so in her mind she clung to the Nurse, who with her vaulting forehead and steely stare Dra— had known for quite some time, though not long enough; and knew she must call the Nurse soon and never speak to the old doctor again.

As if frightened, she hurtled back to the ill-lit, empty bank of hallway telephones and dialed the Nurse's number, heart and limbs thrilling to the thought of the Nurse picking up the old, heavy, buzzing phone and speaking who knew what words, what blank, terse phrases; and Dra— steadied herself then, remembering that the Nurse, so frequently warm, could just as often be stern and snappish. Also worrisome was the prospect that the Nurse might never pick up the call, or that it might be answered by a lackey.

But the Nurse, with her starch-smelling uniform and sure hands, was always more available than a doctor ever was, and the Nurse's appointment slots were far longer than any doctor's. One could stay with the Nurse for an hour and even longer—this being proof that the Nurse was much more thorough than a doctor, for the Nurse fielded questions, waiting long, torturous moments before answering them, and it was important to remind oneself over and over, she recalled, that the Nurse might be crabby at any given time.

Not too long ago, perhaps even while finishing school, Dra— had devised various means of visiting the Nurse, taking advantage of the woman's long appointment slots, and would wind up, for one reason and another, lingering whole afternoons and weekends in the Nurse's office, reading pamphlets, daydreaming and the like while every hour the Nurse would look sternly through the crack in the door, to the satisfaction, it seemed, of them both. Often in those days she made such visits up to two times per week; and one week, she actually went three times. Another time, Dra— purposely skipped appointments, a tack which proved quite effective in ruffling the Nurse's composure; in fact, she became so disturbed that she admitted, through tiny, gritted foreteeth, that she, the Nurse, had grown accustomed to Dra—'s visits and now rather missed them.

And there was no matching the sensation this remark had created, nor the overall excitement of stirring the Nurse's sentiments in various ways. Afterward, Dra— tried often to draw such threads of sentiment from the Nurse, sometimes with subtly rich results, until one day the Nurse grew severely cross and forbade further games—this admonition in itself was gratifying—yet overall, seeing the Nurse was much more gratifying than seeing a doctor, hands down.

The phone rang on, but no one, not even a clerk, picked up the call. Finally she heard a click in the earpiece and a long, sonorous hum, which seemed to indicate something dire, she felt, such as a disaster or death, though it was possible the employees were merely eating lunch. As a matter of course, Dra— knew, the Nurse often left her site to roam pacifically, so her office was frequently under the care of substitute nurses and other coarse helpers who, Dra— knew, were wholly unfit for nursing and generally strayed badly from their tasks.

It was usually best to avoid substitutes, she reminded herself, since after all, there was no substitute for the Nurse, with her stiff, sheetlike face and well-shaped wig. It was always eminently satisfying to hover near her, waiting long hours even for a terse smile. And though substitute nurses had potential, and sometimes offered information about the Nurse herself, they were usually gruff and unfamiliar, or even male.

With these provocative thoughts in mind, Dra—

quickly hung up the hallway phone, knowing very well that she did not want a substitute to pick up the dislodged call, but only the Nurse, the real Nurse; and suddenly she remembered that once, years ago, while detouring through an unfamiliar bank of offices, she had, completely by chance, glimpsed the Nurse staring gloomily through a dark window, hands on hips, wearing only a girdle.

With a pounding throat, she stepped away from the hallway telephone to take several sips of water from a small, capped metal cup which she kept in her skirt pocket and loved. She took the gritty, salty water between her lips thirstily, thoughts on nothing if not the Nurse, and the Employment Office too, for she had not yet presented herself there, though it was not at all far from where she now stood.

The ache, embedded in her back, began to move again, curving with each breath; it had gained in strength, breadth, and plausibility; and seeing that it was at its obvious height, she realized that the best course of action would naturally be to go immediately to the Nurse.

Willfully, she decided that she would like nothing better than to forget about the Employment Office and rush to the Nurse without even making an appointment. This would displease the Nurse, who did not care for unannounced visits. But in the brief and unbearable excitement of planning this visit, Dra— decided she would inform the Nurse and all surrounding staff that planned appointments were destructive and unwise, too; they were artificial, ruinous to those who had urgent needs, and that the best way of staving off emergencies was to see a nurse in an open format, at any time they wished, and oftener.

If she went in search of a late train right now, she might be able to find the Nurse tonight, doing paperwork under a flickering lamp; and merely by laying eyes upon her, Dra— might be struck enough so as to be cured of all ills; but by that time it would be murderously late at night and the Nurse would likely be angry.

Alternatively, she thought, leaning, her back to the wall, she could take the later train and reach the Nurse's quarters after midnight, then settle down quietly to sleep on the Nurse's steps. In either case, once she had stayed the first night, she would surely be able to stay on for second and third nights, not only becoming more calm in general by doing so, but also growing more deeply, ineffably acquainted with the Nurse through protracted, mutually difficult discussions.

Dra— imagined herself sleeping on the steps for several nights in a row, because she would enjoy the tension of being at such a short distance from the Nurse, who, in that scenario, might after all rise from deep sleep at any moment of the night and call out sharply from her bunk that sleeping on the steps was unhealthful, and that Dra— must come inside.

Smiling, scratching the inside of her wrist voluptuously, she wandered toward a lone hallway bathroom, standing dreamily in its damp, unpleasant vestibule for some time, then decided to wait: it was always much better to resist using a bathroom. But due to curiosity, she wound up poking her head through the door anyway, just, she told herself, to have a look inside.

With trepidation, she picked around the bathroom with its broken sinks and toilet bowls filmed inside with dust and grit, and she retrieved, from the clammy base of one, an old, torn pamphlet that listed various employees, long dead, and the worksites where each had worked diligently for years. The page also listed several personality traits for each, and a second column opined as to the pastimes and passions each might have pursued had they been able.

On the long list of names, she saw her own, though prefaced by an unfamiliar single initial; in another portion of the pamphlet, she caught the line of dreamlike letters that formed the name of her new Administrator, a name she had known possibly always, but never heard spoken aloud. Years ago she had come across the name, too—when lying, the whole of one day, upon a stiff, scratchy sofa in the dean's office at school, recovering from anesthesia, so wildly thirsty and out of sorts that she had been unable to think for hours. But gaining her bearings, she had risen on an elbow and pulled from beneath the sofa a dun-colored notebook that listed on its first page the names and phone numbers of a certain colorful tier of Administrators, her own included. Not only this, but next to the name was a photograph of the woman, her mouth open wide in song; and beneath this photo and photos of others, a caption noted wryly that nothing in life could really be proven, not the existence of any person, either, nor the shape of their face nor any detail of their body. Below that, another caption mocked that notion, saying that if people were generally loved and comfortable in life, such ideas would never arise in the first place.

And now, she ran from the bathroom to hide beneath a chamberlike stone stairwell, heart racing with giddiness and frustration over her various fierce, random thoughts about the Administrator and the Nurse both; and she managed to see that if she, Dra—, were extremely lucky, she might somehow develop slow, strong bonds with each of them, so that eventually, they all might grow inseparable; and then she kneeled, due to flashes of nausea.

Still holding the pamphlet in her hand, making an effort to read on, she turned to its back side and saw that its last paragraphs informed as to steps for cleaning limb wounds. Staring at the wall for a few minutes, she concluded that, no matter what else happened, she must see the Nurse, her resolution over this pounding in her head like a gong. Yet peering out from beneath the stairs, seeing the facade of the Employment Office at a distance down the hall, she moved begrudgingly toward it, reassuring herself that afterwards, in no time at all, she would head for the Nurse, and so be able to relax.

She would simply have to find the Nurse later, she told herself, after she had secured a job. Then she would need the Nurse, whose skills were vast, to check her deeply and clean away all unpleasant distresses; but in fact, if she delayed employment now and instead asked the Nurse to open her chest, back, and abdomen in surgery this very night, the Nurse would find something terrible inside her, Dra— knew, quite possibly a sly disease that worked slowly over time to clot and stifle its victims' organs with a kind of gristle. Dra— was fairly sure she harbored this gristle, because years before, Dr. Billy had told her, during a rushed examination performed in a locker without the benefit of electricity, that she had a fair chance of developing it because she was predisposed to it, and because she often ate the wrong things.

She rose and dashed across the main hallway, moving along its far edge, hurrying, resolving not to stop until she reached the door of the Employment Office, though even as she ran, her thoughts returned to the Nurse. The Nurse was often cross and harsh, she reminded herself excitedly, and the Nurse had roomfuls of equipment for treatments, some of which required more nudity than others; and running faster now, Dra— realized just how badly she needed to see the Nurse, that she was practically dying for the lack of it, yet the facade of the Employment Office, with its imposing glass door, now stood before her, and she needed to go in. Afterward, she told herself, she would be able to resume the luxury of thinking about the Nurse's treatments.

Moving toward the ramp that inclined toward the door, Dra— stopped suddenly, stunned, for she saw The Man with No Hair moving across the far end of the ramp, carrying a basket of rubber bulbs. He wore a brown outfit with brown shoe-boots, extraordinarily small, she noticed, as were his hands.

The man stared ahead, no real expression on his face, though it was long-familiar by now, with its snaking nose and bottomless weariness in the eyes; and the familiarity was comforting. In a moment he had entered the office and was out of sight, not before she noticed his hair, which was slightly fuller than she remembered—perhaps it was growing back due to an abatement of illness, she thought; and observing the downy, weak-looking hair growing along the back of his bony skull and past the boundary of his collar, her chest lurched absurdly.

She recalled passing through some uninhabited department long ago—though it could not have been as long ago as childhood—and seeing the man, completely bald, in the same brief, passing manner; he had been sitting beneath a lamp at his bare work table, absolutely motionless, as if unable to stir.

And now the man had gone inside the Employment Office, and she, who needed a job so desperately and had deferred finding one for so long, could not enter, because she could not bear to see him—less from shyness than from embarrassment across a spectrum that included almost everything.

Instead, she ran across the hall to a bank of telephones that faced the office, lifted up the broad, overheavy receiver, and dialed the operator.

It would be simple, she told herself, to ask the operator to connect her with the Employment Office; and she would arrange her new job in this way, over the phone—it was the best she could do. It would work out for the best, anyway: for she now recognized inside herself an enormous longing to speak at length to an operator about great numbers of serious things—which would be a great relief, too, because she had not really spoken lately.

And in a moment when the operator came onto the line, available in so many senses of the word, Dra— would introduce herself, and even perhaps offhandedly describe the man to the operator, and ask if the operator knew him, because the operator might; and heartened, she decided to ask the operator about the Nurse, and job sites, too, and about the thin line separating the gestation of happiness from actual happiness, and the futile enterprise of trying to cling to people who are gone.

As the line clicked open, her heart pounded, for she had no idea how to put all this to the operator, or beyond that, how to tell the operator what she really wanted, deep down; but as it happened, none of this mattered, for she heard the operator talking to someone else, another woman. Dra— hesitated, listening, because in fact the operator was crying.

"It's not true," the operator sobbed, gulping wetly. "But you had to say it, and on my birthday, too!"

"I thought it was important to say," replied the other woman evenly.

"How can you tell such a lie?" the operator said with extreme agitation. "Do you think I'll believe every fool thing you come up with, even to the effect that my mother threw me out like a dead rat? That never happened!" She drew in air noisily. "But even if it did, what would it matter now? That's in the past, and the past is for babies who live there to cry their eyes out!" She broke into sobs again.

The other woman said, "Once you accept the truth, I imagine you will feel hurt and angry; then, you'll begin to feel better."

"Quiet!" the operator screamed. "Angry? Yes, not because of what you say, but only because of my awful half-a-life, with everyone running away the second they say hello or tiptoeing around like they're afraid of the dead!" She burst into tears anew.

"Things are difficult, right now," the other woman said. "People may sense you are having trouble."

"Oooh!" yelled the operator with force. "Why are so many people alive in the first place, can you answer me

that? Why were they all born? How can they all stand
to exist, so filthy with sweat and dust and work, sitting
together on benches like it's the most natural thing in the
world? All that skin flaking away to the ground, turning
to dust, all the hair, think of it! God," she moaned, "think
of feet! No one ever talks about these things, do they?
That's because no one can stand it. Do you know how
many people are in the world?"

"Not really," the woman answered.

"Well, I do, and I'm not going to tell you because the
number might make you sick! What are all these people
doing alive?"

"Well, you're alive," said the woman.

"But I can see into these things better than most
people!" the operator yelled. "Answer me, why do
they continue to live? They're only going to be very
disappointed!"

The other woman gave a deep, slow sigh, which was
followed by the sound of the operator crying, berat-
ing, "Why can't they stop, instead of satisfying God's
wishes?" After which Dra— quietly replaced the receiver,
for the operator was too upset to offer help right now.

Disappointed, Dra— pondered; she could not go into
the Employment Office, not with the man inside, for her
thoughts about him shamed her as much as anything. So
she crouched below the row of telephones opposite the
office entrance to wait until he left. Once he was gone,
she told herself, she would go inside, provided the department was still open; though it was open now, and the
hour was terribly late.

Much later, as she waited in the dead silence of the hall,

she shifted her weight; and then, cramped, she waited a good hour longer, until she felt a vibration and looked up: the Employment Office door swung open and the man appeared, though now in a wheelchair, accompanied by a lean attendant whose eyes fanned back and forth as he slid the chair down the hall.

She waited perhaps an hour longer, just in case the man should be wheeled back; and finally, exhausted, she rose painfully and moved toward the Employment Office door, ready beyond words to settle the business of finding a job. She considered asking the receptionist inside where a fresh drink of water might be found, though she hated the thought of asking for such things and then being rebuffed.

It would not be practical in any case, she realized, to ask for water at this late hour, since the office was probably shut down for the night. So banishing this thought and all others from her mind, she held her breath and pushed through the door of the Employment Office, seeing, to her mild surprise, dozens of workers milling to and fro in the half-lit rear portion of the room, hauling files and papers into a long corridor beyond. To the side of the office, a few employees, perhaps on their breaks, sat on toilets reading newspapers with great absorption, rattling the pages as they readjusted their elbows on their knees.

This sight was somewhat comforting, and she moved toward a niche in the wooden counter where visitors were meant to stand and wait. A woman in a red pleated skirt was sitting at a desk behind the counter, chin in hand, staring at her. The woman said, "Excuse me, but are you in pain?"

Dra— hesitated, not knowing how to answer succinctly, gaping at the woman, who, with her long face, enormous features, and thick, rather insolent stole of hair, now stood, planting her fingertips on the desktop. She stepped forward and introduced herself as the Manager, extending her hand over the counter as if to shake briefly before withdrawing the hand then placing its large palm on the side of Dra—'s neck, as if to check for fever.

"I know you want a job, and that's fine. Beginning right now, you will depend completely on me to help you find one. Does that disturb you? It might. Yet, it's so very common for us to depend on others for our jobs, or even for our sense of self, do you know what I mean? It's true," the woman nodded, smiling for a second, red lips pursed charmingly; "and if our mother did not respond to us warmly when we were young, or if she left us in order to go to the cinema, we probably felt like we didn't exist at all, do you see? Right now, do you feel like you don't quite exist either? As if you've been, perhaps, blown off the face of the earth?"

The Manager strode out from behind the counter, revealing a surprisingly heavy torso, which was odd, for her limbs were exceedingly thin. "Yes, you do feel that way: I can feel it myself, just looking at you. Painful memories are everywhere inside you, dating from your earliest moments—you know, the time when the world was not perfect enough for you? We all have such memories," she giggled, revealing long teeth.

"Now, let's talk about employment," the Manager went on, leaning her elbow on the counter, slipping off a shoe, raising it to peer in and blow inside it. "I commend you on the wish for a job—jobs are tedious and death-making and we can't change that—if we tried to change it, why, there might be an earthquake! Or worse—well, don't think about that, or the future, when we will be dead and gone from ourselves in the strangest way, without bodies. We're much too busy to have time for those thoughts!

"It's hard," the woman said wonderingly, leaning on the counter, "to know who people really are when alive, never mind when they're dead. And as for you, no matter who you are, I don't want to see you wind up working at some horsey old job site where there's no water to drink nor any solid way of life. Do you see? I want you to thrive. And actually, you are lucky. Because today I have some work available—a permanent job, no less!

"There are actually two such jobs open, so you'll need to choose between them," the Manager continued, swiping at her thick bangs. "I allow my employees to choose; it's healthy to choose, isn't it? Choosing is handy; it reflects the fact of our freedoms, and also the fact that every little thing we do has repercussions. Choosing makes sense! Everyone makes choices—there always seem to be so many choices to make; and yet," she began to whisper, "there are really so few after all! Right?" She winked and pulled a tissue from her sleeve, swabbing her nose with it.

She spoke more loudly: "Did you ever notice that some employees try to refrain from making choices, as if wanting to hide from their responsibilities? Those people are in the margins of life—they don't understand that not choosing is but a choice in itself! And that's sad. Why, all actions, even the scantest movements of our eyelids, are choices, and no one can escape that fact." She shook her head. "By God, you're going to choose!" she said huskily, eyeing Dra— carefully. "Now, don't be concerned if you feel a numbness in your limbs—that's only the chill of an open hole before you."

The Manager stood upright, staring not at Dra—'s eyes, but at the base of her neck, as if pinning numerous hopes there.

And Dra—, made eager and enthused by the Manager's speech, clasped her hands together, watching hopefully as the Manager strode to the end of the counter and used her forefinger to indicate the two worksites on a thick wall map, which rustled and undulated and would not lie flat.

These jobs, the Manager was saying, were new jobs, never before offered to any employee; and both were excellent jobs, exciting too, as well as devastatingly lonely, one located at a remote encampment that dealt with the research and classification of dust, and the second at a more centrally located site focused upon the monitoring and maintaining of a small water pump.

The Manager handed Dra— a pamphlet that described the pump station: it would actually present fewer pressures than did other worksites, and there, employees had strong advantages, such as an extra few minutes of rest time for every three and a quarter shifts worked, and flexibility with the identification card.

The card did not need to be worn in full visibility at this site, the pamphlet read, but could be placed casually in any pocket above the waist, so long as an inch of the card showed above the pocket's edge, and if the pocket was too deep, the card needed to be pinned to the pocket, just so the pin was small and neat, and if there was any difficulty in keeping to this rule, the entire pocket would need to be ripped away with a razor, and all other pockets on the employee's person as well, just to ensure that the card always remain exposed and visible.

The Manager smoothed her skirt and took the pamphlet from Dra—, throwing it on the floor. "You will be required to produce your weight in work by the time the probation period has expired—that's routine. I know how badly you want to work, so you'll understand when I say you must hurry and decide which of these jobs you would like. In fact, you need to decide this moment, 'this moment' meaning not only now, but every fraction of time that slips away after this moment, so as you can see, 'now' is really all our futures, and probably part of the past as well. Never mind—if you choose a worksite quickly, you'll be able to escape the burden of uncertainty, at least for a while. Oh, it's always so good to choose—choosing is healthy for the entire body, the newscasters say; why, the very idea of choosing implies release."

The Manager slipped down in her chair, tired, sighing, stretching luxuriously, lifting the weight of her hair behind her neck and musing, "Why is it so hard for you, I wonder? Oh, please, God, you've got to choose. You can't beat choosing. It's best—history tells us so. I like a woman who chooses and who tunes an ear to local protocol—it's an ancient practice amongst females, after all."

She smiled authentically at Dra—, mouth still glossy with the red lipstick.

It was obviously true, Dra— conceded to herself, standing there at the counter, back aching, head pounding with pressure, that choosing would be best; and naturally she wanted a job badly, and yet, neck and face stiff as if paralyzed, she explained to the Manager in quiet, ashamed tones that she could not choose, at least not right now, and with very little movement of the lips she also explained that she did not care which of the two jobs she took, that all she cared for at this moment was to find a corner and sink herself into a deep sleep, because, confidentially, that was what she most loved.

Staring incredulously for a moment, the Manager said, "I don't care in the least what you love! I worked like an animal to find these jobs for you, I did everything, and you have to choose! What would anyone in your place do but choose? Do it now—without any of this ridiculous wavering. Why delay? Choose! The moment you choose, you will be stronger than you are at the present moment; though you might lose something from that moment to this as well. You're lucky to have a choice in the first place, dammit!"

"Ah—" she fumbled.

"Choose, choose right now, for the love of nonsense! God," the Manager fumed, stalking across the room, turning away and saying with intense conviction: "There are two things I hate in this world: those who don't take power when they need to, and those who bend the rules merely for their own comfort. I hate sugar, too," she added with disgust.

Yet it remained that Dra— could not choose, could do nothing but stare far down the hallway where the Manager's employees, faces too distant to make out, were softly sorting through enormous boxes of foam wedges.

The Manager went on, angrier than before, "You can't muster any strength, here, can you: and why not? That's what I want to know, and it kills me, not knowing why. You are a killer, practically; and a killer of choice, too. Why? You are preternaturally lazy, but it's more than that. It's eerie, that's what it is. You're out of touch with things, and I want to know why." She paused, then said with more reserve, "Well, don't worry, we can find out more about you later, with the help of your Administrator and her tools."

The Manager extended her bare heel on the floor, then her toe, before slumping her narrow shoulders in the face of Dra—'s silence and sighing out with great weariness, "Listen! Oh, listen," the scent of her breath complex and troublesome, most likely due to the tremendous strain of this interview, Dra— thought.

"I'm going to let it slide away for the moment," the Manager was saying, "because the most important thing is for you to settle into a job, any job at all. I'll choose for you—how do you like that? And for now, we'll pretend that you made the decision yourself. I said, how do you like that?"

Dra— broke into a sloppy grin as warmth flooded through her, and tears seeped weakly from her eyes as she nodded in pleasure toward the Manager, who looked away with distaste. Sitting at her desk, the Manager then began to search through a large, messy lower drawer.

Several minutes passed, and, still rooting through the papers, the Manager leaned an arm over to unlatch the office gate, motioning with her fingers for Dra— to step behind the counter.

With utter disbelief, Dra— moved through the gate, a floating sensation in her head, and once she stood inside, she tapped at the old wooden countertop and its numerous lower shelves stacked with handsaws just to make certain they were real, since it was so very unusual, unheard of, really, to be invited inside an office gate of any sort; and such an invitation might mean all kinds of things, even the least personal of these being enormously enticing. Standing there, now running her palms across her bristly hair, rattled and excited by everything that had happened, she admitted to the Manager in a burst of pent-up breath how much she was looking forward to her new job, whatever it turned out to be, because she loved the very idea of jobs and steady work, and loved the fact that the world existed just as it did, this world of vast job possibilities and comforting bylaws, and that it was only a temporary nervousness that had prevented her from choosing—for the chance to choose made her feel so important that she had grown dumbfounded and over-come. But the very prospect of having a job signified a vivid turnaround: it meant that life was falling into shape, albeit at this dreadfully late date, but still, she would soon find her niche in life—and while she spoke, she made a mental note to ask the Manager, a few moments hence, for permission to use one of the low, bare toilets along the side wall of the department, since she wanted more than anything to be able to relax, and do all necessary things.

But turning to look, she saw that the Manager sat hunched over the desk, writing with a pen as furiously as if she were preparing a vehement letter of banishment, ignoring Dra— comprehensively.

Staring then at the long, low rows of drawers that lined the nearby room, Dra— spoke on, describing her vigorous enjoyment of errands, and her excitement over certain job privileges she had not yet had the chance to savor, for instance, the stowing away of a cupful of lukewarm water beneath one's desk at night in advance of thirst, or the maintaining of a day file. All in all, she summarized, it was a delight to be here, so very close to finding the job that would finally allow her to blossom.

And finishing these exhortative statements, standing so close to the Manager's desk, excited well beyond normal bounds, she stopped herself from saying any more, thinking, along with what seemed a thousand other thoughts, that these exceptional circumstances—the availability of jobs, the Manager's help, being beckoned behind the counter—all had occurred due to luck, a bounty of it, and, perhaps, by the incredible lateness of the hour, for at this hour, she had heard, Managers often became warm and lax.

Indeed, two jobs were open, and the Manager would choose for her. That itself was cause for quiet reflection, and in these moments she eyed the employees working at the dim end of the passage, their arms now hoisting great bundles of wires, then violently slinging these into open crawlspaces beneath the floors. Smiling, she pondered the difficult decision from which the Manager had released her, and leaned her head against the wall, far beyond exhaustion, closing her eyes.

When she opened them, all the employees were gone, and she saw the Manager standing in shadow at the far end of the silent hallway, gesturing to herself. After some moments the woman swept down the hallway, preceded by a rush of air, and fell heavily into the chair opposite Dra—. "Well?" she asked, a breathless, astonished expression on her face. "What is your decision? Which worksite did you choose? Tell me."

"But I thought you were going to decide for me!" Dra— cried.

"Oh, no, not at all," the Manager replied, chuckling; "I was just trying to relax you by saying that. Come now, you must have decided, in spite of yourself. What is your decision? Tell me now, or write it down on this tab." She waved a piece of cardboard in the air.

Thrown into a sudden overwrought state, twisting her sleeve, despairing now at the idea of ever being able to settle into a real job and into life itself, Dra— scanned the empty office and its hallways, then focused hopelessly on the Manager, who, hair mussed, an advanced look of displeasure on her face, suddenly pitched forward and yelled hoarsely, "Now!" plunging her fist onto the desk.

And Dra—, electrified, looked at the Manager, realizing with swirling emotion that she did not want to find a job elsewhere, not at all, but that she wanted to stay here, here and nowhere else but in this office with the Manager, who was, in fact, so certain of all things and lovely besides; she wanted to work for the Manager; and standing there, waiting for the woman's anger to ebb, Dra— silently mouthed several hopeful words in regard to this, including the Manager's name, which, even without vocal sound, had a strong ring and was full of a filmy, incipient promise.

The Manager leaned forward, furious, pointing a finger, saying, "I am amazed! This is unheard of. You're incapable of choosing, am I to believe that? Tell me!"

"Yes, I suppose," she answered, having scarcely heard the question, instead envisioning a future in which she and the Manager might spend long, calm evenings together, disinfecting hairbrushes and combs.

The Manager folded her hands and thrust them out on the desk with emphasis, saying sternly: "More than anything, I want you to remember that on the last, empty day of your life you will look back in shame over the fact that your existence was ludicrous, a would-be escape, an old flat tire—that is, unless you are able to choose, like everyone else does, right now, this instant."

But no answer came, and in response to this silence, the Manager stood and said gravely, "I want you to go back through this hallway and into one of the closets beyond. You'll see the doors in rows back there, each closet containing a neatly made bed—find one and go in. Shut the door behind you please and turn out the light. Then I want you to get into the bed, urinate fully, and wait quietly for me to come in."

Much, much later, lying in the bed, breathing evenly and somehow with calm, Dra— heard the intermittent sounds of employees returning for the late shift. She heard the Manager's footsteps, too, for she had come to recognize these; and loudly, each with a sharp, cracking sound, they moved toward the closet door, which was then flung open.

The Manager entered the dark room along with a stream of light from the hall that caused Dra— to wince and squeeze her eyes; yet it was possible to see that the woman was now dewy and softly scented, as if fresh from a bath; and with damp hair, bending tenderly over Dra—, she delivered a kiss, breathing, "I believe in finding a job as I believe in nothing else in this life. I believe in a mug of water at the work desk, in a clean, uncluttered working surface, and in the thirty-second break. What I want most is for you to begin a new life with no bumps or joyrides—just work, moving along in a great, flowing, never-ending keel. Do you know—" She paused, eyes shifting indecisively, "I can almost be myself with you! Isn't that funny? I'm saying this only because you have hurt me to the point that I had to die and then come back in order to go on with life. But there it is. 'Why can't she choose?' I asked myself over and over. I ran in circles, seemingly, I pinched myself, I sought the advice of colleagues—why shouldn't I reveal all of this to you now, since there is virtually nothing left of me? Look at the hour! There's no later hour than this, and it's a miracle that we are awake!

"Can it be that you still haven't made a decision, you still haven't uttered a word, though I am being as honest and down-to-earth as I can be? It's no game; don't you know that choosing is the very basis for life, even at the molecular level? What are you waiting for?" She paused, pursing her mouth. "You're wondering who I really am, and what is inside my heart—aren't you? Well, yes, you have a right to know."

They stared at one another.

"But it's really impossible for you to know who I am, and I you," the Manager said downtroddenly. "Oh,

I ache for the passage of time! This is all new to me, you see, this business of being open and honest as a dog." Her energy now seemed depleted; and Dra— observed with a small thrill in her abdomen that this affect was every bit as appealing as the Manager's more commanding side.

"I've never been so lenient with anyone in my life," the woman half-whispered. "But your feelings are causing funny feelings inside of me, and that's strange. I don't like it! You've got to choose!" The Manager shredded some tissue between her fingers, then broke from the room, pulling the wooden door shut behind her.

Dra— lay in the darkness for long hours, thinking of nothing, hearing nothing; presently, though, she began to notice the sounds made by hordes of employees arriving to work for the next shift, including soft footsteps, sliding doors, voices bringing forth fearful, hushed, lukewarm greetings—all the dozens of sounds that issue from an office in the earliest morning hours—along with the smeared-sounding whisper of a woman: "Thank Christ for the silence of night!" coupled with the sound of the Manager's voice screaming brokenly, perhaps over the telephone, "Damn it all to hell!" Dra—, eyes closed, considered that the previous hours may have been so trying for the Manager that she, the Manager, might soon break down entirely, which naturally would be Dra—'s fault. After it was all over, however, the Manager might then relent and assign Dra— a job, any job, without requiring her to choose. If that actually occurred, Dra— thought, then luck would truly be with her; so, hopeful, she half-rose from the deep bed, head spinning from the stuffy room and its scent of medication.

Not much later, the Manager burst into the closet doorframe again, bright light behind her throwing her body into silhouette. "Time to join the world!" she cried enthusiastically, moving close, rather bent. The Manager then murmured that a job actually had been found, and that Dra— had been assigned to it summarily, so she must pack immediately and meet her new job Administrator at the train station. After this, she would be ready to report to work.

Bottomlessly relieved, confused and overwarm, Dra— fell back into the bed, clutching the blanket, exhaling, nearly smiling, though she noted that the Manager was now quiet, and that her eyes might have been red as she gazed sadly at the bed, emitting a small sound of grief, as if she were watching over someone with a deep illness that was at last giving way to death.

Slowly the Manager leaned her cheek upon the wooden bedpost, and gave a groaning sigh. "They say all people want the same things," she said with wonder. "Closeness to others, drinkable water—can it be true? Are we all so alike? Is there any way for friends to depend on each other without feeling betrayed and angry enough to jump off a bridge? Why, no, I'm afraid not," she concluded, grinning weakly, closing her eyes.

"Now you'll be leaving!" the Manager cried with sudden new force. "But look how we've grown accustomed to one another, even to one another's scent, in such a short time!"

"I don't think that's true," Dra— muttered, turning her face into the pillow, mind aswarm with dozens of disparate shreds of uncomfortably intimate thoughts.

The Manager said, "There's a little person inside me who gets awfully sad when an employee finally takes a job. Oh! That little person feels helpless and lies on her bed so inert—why, just the way you're lying there now!—but no one comes to help!"

Again the Manager leaned over the bedclothes. "I just loathe life when people go off to worksites all on their own and leave me," she said hopelessly. "Leaving is like a terrible seduction, but a different kind of seduction, a falling into the ground, a humiliation that one is power-less to drive away! Oh, sure, I have my job to do, and I do it," she added flatly. "Still, what am I but a girl?"

"Ah—" said Dra— uneasily, voice muffled by the blanket.

"Tell me, how much do you like me?" the Manager whispered, bending low, sidling along the bed-frame.

"I don't know."

The Manager expelled a snorting breath and her tone hardened. "That's all you can say? Never mind then, you're going to change like hell when you meet your new Administrator, believe me. And listen—" A wily look passed through her eyes and she bounced the bed enthusiastically with her palms, grinning. "You won't recognize yourself when it's all over! You'll be all differ-ent, not like now, and every single day of your life from then on you'll be making decisions by the mountainful! Won't that be wonderful?"

"No!"

The Manager turned to regard herself in a small hand-mirror. "Look at me, I'm as tough as a whistle! I'm not losing," she said softly, wiping her hand down her hip with great pleasure. "I'm doing just fine, and sometimes I forget that."

She strode to the door, smiling. "I do hope you like your new job; it's a complex job, I hear, one that's inextricably bound up with the future, so you'll probably want to bring a headscarf. You'll be working at the pump site, dear."

The Manager crushed her palm upon a wall switch, causing the room to blaze with light, and the scars and holes of its homely wooden walls were revealed.

"And also," the Manager paused dramatically, blinking, "I know you're anxious to meet your new Administrator. Well, let me tell you all about her right now: she's a real dream. You'll meet her at the train station, do you understand?"

Then the Manager slowly pronounced the Administrator's full name, including her maiden name; this Dra— took in with excited, fearful eyes, and she sat up, pulse rising, now more than ready to leave the room.

"You're afraid of others' feelings, aren't you?" the Manager said, eyes focusing hard on the bed. "You're afraid of anger. Why? I can see it in your face—you'd do anything to avoid anger, even stop defecating, wouldn't you? Oh, dammit,"—her voice rose again—"who will be left to talk to me? There's no one here, not really. Don't I want a steady friend to help and hurt me just like everybody else? Tell me, why is it so hard to need another woman, after all?"

Huge, sentimental tears rolled down the Manager's face, and Dra—, pained on her behalf, waited patiently, for the Manager had grown so candid and warm in these few moments that indeed the thought of leaving her and this entire office—she had been here at least three days—caused her enormous grief. She flopped back into the bed, staring at the slanted ceiling, struck with awe, for even in this moment of silence, the Manager's voice rang miraculously in her ears, and the Manager's long face with its bright red lipstick was fixed in her mind.

And the Manager, so attractive in her various skirts and dresses, might indeed have been the ideal boss, but there was no hope of working here with her, Dra— realized: that would be a shameful thing to do, because the only valid, real task was to find her Administrator and begin work at the pump site, never turning away from that. And so, clamping her feelings shut, Dra— whimpered once then turned over in the bed. The Manager opened the door of the closet, and with a hollow sob disappeared deep within the matchstick hallways far at the rear of the department.

After an hour or so of silence and no sign of the Manager returning, Dra— finally rose from the bed, heavy-hearted, body and clothes rather damp, and padded from the closet, searching fruitlessly for the Manager.

But the Manager was gone, she realized, passing rows of abandoned lockers, buckets filled with doorstops, and a small pot of soured soup on the floor; then she came upon a small changing room near the filing cabinets, its walls laden with blurry photographs of ignominious employees dating from decades past. She scanned the images of the worn faces, envious, for these people obviously had worked successfully and without incident for dozens of years on end; yet she turned and banished all such wishful notions from her mind and toweled off, changing into a fresh skirt.

Now in the waiting area, she held before her a lengthy note from the Manager, which she had found nailed to the countertop. The note detailed the time Dra— was to meet her new Administrator at the train station, and also the topics that the two of them should probably discuss, including the problem of maintaining physical integrity in the face of friendship, and various conundrums involving intimacy and telephones. They ought also to discuss grades of paper stock, the note instructed.

But Dra— could not absorb all the note's information, and stuffed it into her skirt pocket, instead thinking fondly of the winsome, fickle Manager and all the things she had said. She moved toward the front counter of the darkened office, then, still dreaming, leaned her head there heavily until her attention was caught by an enormous old book lying nearby.

The book seemed to be a descriptive index of all jobs everywhere, charting and cross-referencing them in so many dozens of ways that it seemed, she thought, beginning to flip through, ludicrous—as was the book's gnatlike print which grew smaller and smaller as the chapters progressed, until it disappeared into the grain of the paper itself.

Skipping the long preface, she glanced upon an advisory written by the book's editor, warning that if some employees were insubstantial and weak, it only meant that they imagined an overpowering entity in their vicinity, and that it was this noisome frame of mind, in which a party was so fearful that they could not assume full responsibility for self, which was the major cause of suffering.

Fretting, she turned further into the book and unexpectedly caught sight of a reference to her new job, one minute digging avidly into the pages to locate the tiny paragraph and read it, the next sitting down on the floor to cry in disappointment, for the chief of the two listed job duties was the spooning of unhealthy human hair from the floor into refuse containers filled with a strong fluid.

Yet it was later, exhaling, resting on a gray institutional couch near the door, that she began to think in earnest about her new job and its place in the world, realizing that all work, if viewed with a clear gaze, was in fact important, if not actually key—key in the sense that the tiniest bolts ultimately bear up the frame of a machine so it can continue to function, even in the event of a trauma. So it was with this thought, and so many other positive thoughts just like it, that she finally pushed through the door and left the Employment Office in search of her Administrator, who certainly would greet her with warmth and teach her all sorts of valuable new skills, so that she, Dra—, could finally begin to live at the point at which most lives typically begin.

Walking according to the directions on the sheet, she wound through an unfamiliar hallway, hearing the hollow whirring of machinery, then pressed onward, climbing a block of padded stairs. At the top she found herself at the entrance to a huge storehouse cluttered with upright rolled metal, and looking in, she gasped with surprise, for The Man with No Hair was passing through the other end of the room, pouring pills from a brown bottle into his mouth.

Heart racing, she fumbled to a nearby empty work desk and sat, breathing hard, wanting badly to follow the man and speak to him; yet she was unable. Soon, when she was settled into the job, she reasoned, she would probably be speaking to him quite frequently, in any case, with ease and confidence, too. Perhaps they would pass notes to one another in the hallway as their paths crossed, or, she also imagined, walk together in search of water, maybe even finding some.

Yet these imaginings sickened her to the point that she leaned over and weakly spat onto the floor, since what exactly she would say to the man—who knew what words, what impossible sounds—was inconceivable, as was the idea of growing deeply familiar with his entire person, loose belt and pallid demeanor included. So she realized quickly that if they ever so much as spoke, she would need to put an end to it immediately.

Sitting there at the empty desk, she grimly put the man from her mind and again uncrumpled the assignment sheet, which informed that she was to work at many, many jobs from now on, not only the pump site; and that these adjunct jobs, though menial, were scattered throughout a wide range of floors and departments; the sheet also described how all jobs were connected, and supported the same convictions. Reading on, Dra— dropped off to sleep, then woke reading the last line of the sheet, which said she must report to one of these adjunct jobs twenty minutes hence, at a site not far from here.

She got up and ran briskly toward this site, paying

heed to the sheet's directions, which pinpointed a spot on the far side of a roof, accessible only via a series of elevators. She knew these elevators and had ridden them before: ill-lit inside, they leaned topside forward as they shot upward, then curved in jagged patterns along the sides of high walls before depositing passengers and returning to their final station, where they were serviced by mechanics in gas masks.

The dark, miles-long roof was covered by another roof and so on, the top roof being unreachable in all ways; and as she walked toward the elevators, she passed a small niche that contained an open-walled guard station, though it did not contain a guard, but instead two figures struggling unpleasantly beneath a cloak, and she turned away.

Once upon the roof she saw, at a short distance, hundreds of small indoor airplanes in rows, engines roaring powerfully, as hundreds of employees waited at a distance to board them. Through a haze of smoke, she watched the small planes taking off and landing every few moments, scorching past her so closely, in fact, that her body vibrated enjoyably.

Amidst the deafening noise, the employees stood quietly in lines, some nearly naked, some wearing thin gray woolens or other haphazard-looking clothing. Stepping past an old mechanically driven clock that leaned crookedly, she realized that at this time of day employees generally left their work shifts for other, longer, more complex work shifts that would last far into the night and for days beyond that.

In one of the lines she observed a man of young middle

age wearing only a tan, collared shirt and socks, the skin of his scalp mottled and exposed. He grasped anxiously at his thighs, squinting in the murky air, then, hesitating, he stepped over and reached out to tap the elbow of the woman next to him, who was older and wore dark kneesocks and a tattered coat. The man smiled at her and over the noise called loudly, "I see you're tired, probably bone-tired, and I just want to say that I feel that way, too! It looks like life is hard for you right now, and I hope that's true — I mean, I hope you're just like me, but I can't presume. Or can I?"

The woman, face terse, blank, stared ahead. "What are you talking about?" She turned to look at him, and he ducked and smiled.

"Here comes your airplane," the woman said loudly. "Go on with the others!"

The man called out, "I always say the wrong thing!"

"The wrong thing?" the woman mocked. "If you think I'm saying you're wrong and I'm right, then you're imbuing me with authority I don't have! I'm nobody's mother. Now, walk over there to that little plane!"

"Oh," the man said weepily, stepping up to her. "The truth is, I've never flown to a new worksite before — I've never flown at all!"

"Is that right?"

"Yes! And now, my Administrator has expelled me for eating — eggshell, that is, and I have to go away on a plane! She doesn't want me anymore — that's the point. I should have fought her, I should have refused to leave, but I didn't!" he said, bending to one side, as if with a cramp. "In the most crucial moments, I always fail to act!"

"Of course you fail to act," the woman said, a hint of gaiety in her eyes.

"I don't want to fly! I'm afraid of disaster, but I'm also afraid of diverting disaster!" the man said, letting forth a gulping, nervous laugh, his face filling up with bright pink.

A plane rose into the air nearby amidst deafening noise, then floated away. "Isn't all of life an accident, anyway?" the woman said mildly.

"I may sound unreasonable, but my nerves make me this way. It's just nerves," the man said, looking around.

"We all hate to fly," the woman said. "Oh, how we hate it, but we fly anyway, don't we? 'We fly to work, we fly onward,' as the saying goes, and as another saying goes: 'If you don't mind waiting in line for a plane, I doubt anyone else does either!'"

"When is the right moment to state my demands? What is the best moment to disagree with someone?" the man broke out. "I can't seem to find that moment, yet it must exist! Is it best to refuse another person's ideas point-blank, with no room for discussion? Perhaps in the case of parties, I should leave quickly, before they ever start!"

A small plane rolled toward their line, bumping past, engines gunning. The man cried out, terrified, and tried to turn away as the woman pushed him forward, shouting into his ear, "That's your plane! Stop fighting it, will you? It makes me sick to see people like you, so without dignity."

The man staggered toward the bright body of the plane and fell to his knees, crying, as the woman stepped back with a smirk, her fist clenched in the air in a gesture of goodwill and departure. "Goodbye!"

The man turned beet-red, screaming uncontrollably as a nimble pilot leapt from the plane, laughing good-naturedly and waving to the woman. He hauled the crying man into the plane's compartment and slammed the door. Appearing in the window, the man motioned to the woman in panicked gestures that she should come toward the plane, but instead she stood rocking on her heels as the plane shot down the runway, bumping and bucking until it lifted from the roof and into the haze.

By now, most of the employees had gone to their next work shifts. Standing near the runways, breathing in deeply the black waste of the planes, Dra—, hair blowing stiffly back, watched the woman stroll away, hands in pockets, head down, smiling to herself. In the distance, planes landed, then rolled toward openmouthed tunnels near the edge of the roof where they paused, then plunged, heading for small, lighted stations so far below they were nearly invisible.

From a stairwell door, two well-dressed women emerged. They walked across the roof holding hands, speaking intensely and zealously to one another as if they had recently spent a close period of time together and guarded the experience viciously. Sitting on two summer chairs alongside a cement pillar, the women squinted in the dust as they discussed some third party, and Dra— modestly moved out of their view.

"I know who you mean, and she's a terrible liar," the thinner woman said, sitting on the edge of her chair.

"Yes, yes, I know! I don't really like her, either, but

that's just me, I suppose," said the other.

"Well, you're nothing like her, Marla, not at all. You're as far from her as you can get from the moon, except you are fiercely loyal as a friend. I've heard that she is loyal, too."

"Oh, she's not loyal, I bet, not at all—she's just a big tub of nothing!" the first woman said, grinning hugely. "You're so different from her, Slim! You're clever, you have such spark!"

Her friend smiled. "Clever—yes, you have described me. I also happen to know that she, for all her loyalty, has not a fraction of your native talent, Marla."

"Oh, you're flattering me!" the stockier woman said, blushing. "I've loved this entire day! I love being with you, Slim. When we talk, I get the feeling that nothing will ever go wrong!"

"So feeling secure is very important to you," the other woman said, eyes wandering. "I wonder why?"

"I don't know," Marla said. "I just know that I feel linked to you somehow. I can't explain it but I know it's true. How can I bother with my old friends anymore? They don't understand me the way you do, they're not in the same mental league. They're such silly, stupid girls."

"Life is easy for people who have the luxury of being silly and stupid, isn't it?" Slim said, lying back, smiling assuredly, arms extended on the chair's armrests.

"That's just what I think!"

"And being less aware, those people are unable to recognize their own disadvantages to begin with."

"Oh—it's fascinating, listening to you, Slim," said Marla, with an appearance of trying to suppress elation.

"Do you know how everyone is a little in awe of you? The other girls talk about you at night, you know — and here I am, speaking with you for the second time in my life! And, I want to ask you — "

"Yes?"

"It's just something I've been wondering," Marla said, and paused. "I want to be your client!" she burst forth, flushing terribly.

"Ah, the whole world wants to be my client," Slim laughed, flexing her fingers, "and so do you, naturally. But you are not my client, Marla, you are my student. That fact is unalterable. I can teach you, I can speak, I can listen, but you will never be my client. That would be inappropriate."

"But this is different!" cried Marla. "You would make an exception for me, because we are already so close!"

"That's exactly why it's a bad idea. You're asking for the impossible, do you see? Really, Marla, I think this wish of yours bears some deeper examination."

Marla began to cry. "Don't humiliate me for another second!" she said stickily. "I should never have bothered being honest with you!"

"Dear, I think it's interesting that you think I am humiliating you when I am simply telling you what I will and will not do."

Marla put her hands over her ears and in large, clumsy movements ran across the roof, shouting crossly at Slim, who, still sitting in her chair, cast a careful, absorbed gaze upon Marla.

"I expressed my feelings!" Marla turned and shouted from across the roof. "You told me to do that, so I did!

And now, you're punishing me for doing it! You're ruining me!"

"Oh—Marla!" Slim said, holding out her arms. "Just a few minutes ago we were so close! Stop it and come back here, dear. You're only embarrassing yourself by conjuring up dramas long dead."

"You witch!" Marla yelled, scarlet with rage. She ran far across the roof toward the noisy airstrips and the planes, which dwarfed her.

Slim called across the roof, "Marla, what are your thoughts about your mother?"

"What?" Marla called, tiny.

"I am not your mother!" Slim yelled. "I am your teacher and friend, but right now, I'd like you to tell me something about your mother. Tell me her most distinct characteristic."

"I don't feel like it! Why should I, when the truth is you don't care?"

"That's silly, Marla. Why did you ask to be my client? Only because you know I care."

Marla paused. "Is that a riddle?" she asked, squinting, fussing with her hair, separating it into tufts.

"Well, yes, in a way! It's your riddle, Marla."

"I don't know."

"Oh, come back, you silly, lazy girl," Slim called with pleasure.

Scuffling back across the roof, Marla whined, "But I want to be your client!" as she grasped Slim's dry fingers and slid into her arms.

Slim took Marla's embrace, pulling her onto her lap, looking at her closely. "I assure you that you are not my client. Do you realize we were involved in a struggle just now? And struggle is part of life, do you know that? Why, sometimes, it's just what the doctor ordered!" She coughed raspingly. "Now, say this: You are my teacher—"

"You are my teacher," Marla said.

"Good." She paused. "And as your teacher, I can't help but notice that you often behave in a contrary, even seductive manner, Marla, and—do you know what—I am also beginning to think that struggle titillates you," she said, smiling a little, eyes moving to the distance. "All this is worth examining, isn't it?" She waited. "Struggle titillates her," she murmured.

"Oh, I don't know," sighed Marla, rubbing her head with her hands. "I hate fighting, but all the same I love it. I know I don't know how to explain it, but—" she sighed. "Fighting is heaven, when it's over, I mean." She pushed her face into Slim's shoulder.

"Marla—"

"I want to be your client, so you can—don't you see? I'm thirty-two years old, and I deserve some pleasure, dammit!"

Presently she slumped over, asleep, releasing her weight upon Slim, who sighed, draping her arm over the silver-haired Marla.

Slim leaned down to rummage through her purse and pulled out a box of sucking candy. Placing a piece in her mouth, she lisped to the sleeping woman, "There are theories galore about attachment and most of them are silly. Instead of all that, I like to say, 'You may have strong feelings, but they have little to do with reality!' Or, 'When you are angry at another person, it's all about you, no one else, so think, think hard about your conflicts, and only if you're lucky will the wind blow you away!'"

She shook Marla. "Wake up! I don't like sleeping people. Sleep is a barrier between folks and for what reason? None. Why should I have imaginary conversations with you when you could just as easily be awake, talking to me?"

She took another candy, looking at Marla's closed eyelids, small and scaly-red. "Do you know what I think? I think the best part of life is merging with others. Oh, some think it's bad, but then, they don't really know how to do it correctly! I think deep down, we all want to merge. Two merging into one is perfection; I would defend that idea to my death, and I don't even know why! Let me tell you: I love the beginnings of merging, when clients start to grow attached to me. Trust is planted then, and I see that willing, willing expression in their eyes!"

Marla woke and put her chin on Slim's shoulder. "Should I?" she muttered.

Slim seemed not to hear. "Perhaps I am a glutton! I never seem to have enough merging in my life. Why not? Am I all alone? I don't want to be." She expelled a massive breath and shut her eyes. "Of course, my newest client will merge with me, too: she has no choice, since she is unable to have a relationship with anyone, so, for the moment, I am the only person in the world to her."

Dra—, listening closely, standing a few feet away, now stepped back, suddenly fearful that she herself was this client but somehow did not yet know it. Slim saw her move behind the post, and gave a start.

"What on earth is that?" Slim said, standing, spilling

Marla from her lap. "Don't move, dear," she called out. "We've already seen you. Come here immediately; you may be in sharp trouble. Who are you?"

Anxiously, Dra— stepped forward and explained that she was on her way, though very late, to her very first job assignment, and that things being as complicated as they were, she had stopped along the roof to watch the indoor airplanes, and to think and gain her composure; and now she would be on her way to work at once.

Looking down, Slim began rummaging through her bag again for some moments, as if she had become completely uninterested in this matter, then, lifting her face, she smiled brightly. "Do you know that it's a terrible thing to wander the hallways and rooftops on foot the way you do? It looks bad. Much better to take an airplane to work: your whereabouts will be known at all times then, and you'll meet more people that way, too!" She looked to Marla. "Marla, I think I've seen this young woman before somewhere, probably in some corner with a man."

"Oh, no, no, that's not true," Dra— said quickly, blushing hard, then blushing a second time as she noticed Slim's elegant face and attractive dress; she also noticed that Slim had odd, roaming eyes and did not seem quite to see or hear what was in front of her.

"Don't lie to me, dear," said Slim, as Marla looked on, rather agitated. "I'm not accusing you of anything terrible. I merely assume that everyone I meet has very special, intimate relationships, just the way I do."

"Most of us only want someone to spoil and caress," said Marla.

"Oh, Marla," exhaled Slim. She turned to Dra— and snapped her fingers. "I just know I've seen you with a man, I'm sure of it, but I can't remember who it was, or when. Come, tell me who he is!" Slim prodded. "Are you really comfortable with him at all times, and I mean that in the most delicate sense? My guess is that you are not." Slim paused. Airplanes buzzed in the distance, and a scant breeze blew across the roof.

At this quiet juncture, Dra— realized how terribly late she was for her new job, though she also wanted to stay with these appealing women; and it occurred to her suddenly that she had seen Marla once before, long ago, alone in an elevator, smiling fearfully at a guard.

Slim turned. "Marla, go and watch the airplanes; I want to speak with this young woman alone."

"What?" Marla said, stricken.

Slim said, "It seems you want to hold onto me, Marla, and I see you grow jealous easily. What does that mean? It means you don't like to share, because you feel you'll be cheated—so ultimately, you will never really know the joys of merging. Isn't that rather a problem? It has a name."

"I don't like hearing you talk this way!"

"Go and watch the airplanes, Marla."

Ashen, Marla went, looking across the flat distances of the roof, her skirt rippling in the air.

"You know," said Slim, turning, smiling warmly, enclosing her dry hand around Dra—'s, "I love to learn about others, learn everything I can. Call it a tic: that's just me. I want to learn about you because you're quiet, you see. That draws me in. How would you like to let me be a listener, a confidante, a helper? Sometimes people are terrified to reveal the threads of their innermost feelings — you are this way — but you know, I love those little threads more than anything in this world. I catch them with my fingers! Sometimes people are so terrified of the truth that there is nothing to do but take those threads and yank them, hard and harder, until the truth jumps out! You see, if you allowed me to be a listener, you would learn all about yourself and life. Say yes, won't you? It won't be like other relationships, I promise, it will be unique in a way you've never imagined. Oh, isn't it fate that our spirits will meld together this way? It hasn't occurred yet, mind you; it won't for a few days. We believe in spirits, don't we? Spirits meld to one another easily, because they are made of metal." Slim paused to glance at Marla, who stood quietly nearby, grief-stricken.

Slim drew a breath. "Supposing I learn all the most personal, intimate things about you — as if looking right down into your body. And suppose I take hold of those threads that are wound tight around your heart, choking it." Her voice cracked. "Wouldn't it be wonderful? My profession is based upon a form of love, you know."

"Oh," breathed Marla, shutting her eyes.

"Won't you be my client?" Slim asked Dra—. "Why, you already are, in a way."

"She isn't!" said Marla furiously.

With some confusion, Dra— asked, "Are you talking about a new way to live?"

"Goodness, I'm talking about a way to be together!" Slim exhorted, reaching to hold Dra—'s waist in her hands. "Do you know that there is a terribly fine line between the need to be private and the need for companionship?" she asked.

"No."

"I don't like that line, myself. It irks me. Doesn't it irk many of us?" she asked them both.

"Stop talking!" said Marla.

"Some like to flee," continued Slim. "Don't flee, though I can see that you usually flee. Don't," she said sweetly, now taking Dra—'s wrist.

Marla edged toward them. "I know all about the stuff of relationships. I have knowledge of — "

"Quiet!" Slim said, moving her hands to the top of Dra—'s head, closing her eyes with feeling as she slowly leaned forward and worked her fingertips into the scalp, massaging.

"Let me tell you the story of my life," Slim said, her hands still enmeshed in the hair. "Long ago I was born embattled. Naturally I withheld everything from my mother — my words, and of course my feces. But now, years later, look at me! I am a professional twice over, and an expert to such a degree that you only stand to gain from our liaison. If only you would chance it!" She whimpered softly.

Marla shouted upwards to the domed roof, "Slim, I don't like this, and I'm starting to forget just who and where I am! I'm afraid."

Slim turned to look at Marla, and they were all silent for some minutes. A faint, continuous roar, perhaps airplanes, perhaps only the sound of the vast space enclosed by the roof far above them, could be heard.

"There are hurdles to intimacy," Marla said rotely.

"Yes, that's right, there are hurdles," Slim returned, releasing Dra—'s hair, slowly smiling. "Hurdles there are, there can be, but we overcome hurdles, don't we, Marla!" She laughed and threw her arm around Marla, who smiled back redolently, blinking. "Oh," sighed Slim, turning closely toward Dra—. "Won't you say yes? I know my way around intimacy; I've helped so many people achieve it, too, even in the saddest of cases! Why, for example, even women who shun intimacy as a rule may finally desire it when they learn they are going to die." She drew the chair up again and sat.

"Die?" asked Dra— anxiously. "Which women are going to die?"

"Why, all the sick ones, of course," Slim answered plainly. "It's their own fault, or so the news says."

"They're dying? From what?" she asked.

"From exposure, my dear, exposure! You know—to the poisons of their worksites, to the people close to them—aren't our deepest feelings known to be poisonous as well?

"Women especially are vulnerable to such exposures." Slim's voice trailed off for a moment as she stared, lost in thought; then she resumed in tones of goodwill: "Oh, you'll see how it is—most of us can scarcely maintain spinal health, let alone overall health! We fall to exposure, then sink with the disease." She smiled with unconcern and reached deep into her coat pocket.

Whispering, nearly ill with anxiety, Dra— asked, "Which disease are you talking about?"

"Oh, come, come, must I spell it out for you?" was the curt answer.

Marla piped, "I know the ins and outs of intimacy; I know about desire and constancy, and what it takes for—"

"Yes, she knows," Slim remarked, squinting, lighting a small cigarette. "Marla has a talent for comprehending these things—but of course, so do I, that's why I recognize the talent in her. Marla has intuitive powers I could never have guessed at, either—but part of intimacy is surprise, isn't it? Touché!" She laughed roughly. "We pulled quite a few surprises from Marla, didn't we?"

"I'm suspect, too," Marla said gaily. "I've learned how suspect I am."

"Yes, she is suspect, though half the time, she's suspected of being good—you never know which way it will turn!" Slim laughed, rubbing Marla's shoulder. "She has hundreds of conflicts too—she carries them in her body, left over from you-know-what!"

"Hah!" Marla laughed stiffly.

"But don't you think," Slim went on, suddenly absorbed, "that if the object of love is sensitive, and responds to our anger, then we leap into hope? I think we do! What else is there but this hope? Oh," she sighed, tapping her fingers together, looking tenderly into the distance, "We all want the opportunity to make things right, we want that most of all, don't we?"

With emotion, Marla inhaled and closed her eyes.

Presently, she opened them and said to Dra—, "What about the man?"

"Oh, yes, yes, the man!" Slim stabbed the cigarette out and snuggled into the chair. "I'm interested—who is this man?"

About to say that the women were mistaken, and

that there was no man, Dra— stopped herself, for this would have denied them their powers of acuity; instead she explained softly and with very little breath that at all costs she must leave right now to find her new worksite, because she was vastly, scandalously late, and for this she would surely suffer when her new Administrator got wind of it.

"But it's interesting that you want to leave at this particular moment, just when we are talking about men, and hence, intimacy and gratification. Isn't that interesting, Marla? Gratification recalls conflict, you know."

"We are all drawn to conflict," sang Marla, "every last one of us."

"Oh yes," Slim agreed. "We love conflict, for conflict suggests intimacy. You love conflict; so did Job. I only wish you would face these problems of yours, and let me help! Won't you? Shouldn't you do that before you grow into young middle age and slowly begin to die?"

It seemed a great deal of time had passed.

Slim continued, "I think the truth is that whenever you begin to grow close to someone, you simply crumble like a little teacake, don't you, dear? Marla!" she called sharply, for Marla was wandering toward the far periphery of the roof.

"I empathize, I really do," Slim said softly as Marla raced joyfully back to them, "I know that dreadful sensation of falling apart never really abates, does it? Though over a period of, say, fifteen minutes or so, it may ebb slightly—time enough for a physical experience, at least."

As Marla returned, Dra— stood quietly, pondering her new job and her lateness, so uncomfortable over the things Slim had said; and after some time, as Slim continued to talk and Marla to seek attention, Dra— felt the slow beginnings of a cramp in her abdomen and begged to be excused.

Embarrassed to call attention to herself in this way, she nevertheless left the two women, making quickly for the toilet, a cabinet-sized shack several paces off. Reaching the bathroom's slatted, makeshift wooden door, she peered inside and immediately felt warm and glad, for next to the toilet was a small chair, presumably where a second party might sit in order to give assistance or hold a hand.

After some time, she returned from the bathroom to Slim and Marla, full of a secret, overbearing pleasure about one thing, though regarding another matter, feeling gravely disappointed.

Slim was waiting for her, arms crossed, fingering her long neckscarf. "During this short separation, you've been in my thoughts and I know I've been in yours. But overall, I'm beginning to lose interest in you. You are so inexpressive! I need more stimulus than you offer, since I am lavish in my passions and expressions, so vivid, and you are, well . . ." she trailed off for a moment, then added somberly, "The truth is that I am quite disappointed with the world and all its people, including you."

Slim picked up her coat, a heavy brown fur, saying, "You are quiet, you see, and I make a habit of avoiding quiet people, for the obvious reasons." She reached out a quivering hand. "Yet," she said slowly, thinking, "part of me wants to save you from senseless waters. I crave so many things! Like the special feeling that can only come from one person saving another—so—" She paused. "In a sense, you could say that I've searched the world for you!" Slim laughed, eyes full of tears. "And I would like to make you happy. Oh, don't be nervous, I'm not going to do anything but hold your hand."

Trembling, Dra— let out a sputtering, excited rush of air, scarcely able to imagine what would happen if she were to stay here with Slim, and do just as Slim liked. Yet she was abominably late for the new job, the worry over this rocking inside her foully until, staring at the two women, who were beginning to seem somewhat unreal, she controlled her feelings and stated that at all costs she must leave immediately for her new worksite, or else things would surely take a turn for the worse.

But after making this statement, she merely continued to stand before them, for the very idea of pulling herself away from the two women with their rich clothing and strangely vibrant looks filled her with savage despair.

As the silence went on, Slim sighed and stooped to pull a small telephone from beneath one of the chairs; and as immediately as she raised the phone to her ear, she began speaking warmly to someone.

Marla, arms folded, took this opportunity to step closer and whisper:

"Do you know what it is to say the words, yet not be heard? It rankles, it does! What to do when the other person just doesn't listen? Nothing, you do nothing. We can't change other people and that's that. We hate to speak up anyway because we don't want the pain of a real confrontation, do we? Isn't it easier to sit still and nurse one's thoughts, trying to gain strength to sit for even longer? There's no room for two sides of an argument, either. One side always emerges the winner, doesn't it?"

" Yes," Dra— said, with a crushing rush of empathy.

"And we can't ever assume our friends will understand why we're upset, can we?" Marla shook her head. "I hang in there no matter how I feel, even if it's a gray, awful feeling. Do you? Are you the sticking sort? I am. I'm a good cook and I stick around. I'm older than I look. People who can't stick around aren't really cut out for a relationship."

Finished with the phone call, Slim stood and pulled Marla by the shoulder, drawing her back, as Marla whispered on, "I bet you know what it's like to be depressed and have all sorts of awful, negative thoughts that just coincidentally happen to be true."

Slim said, "Stop talking, girls. Marla and I have places to go, and so we say goodbye. We're off to eat. Tamales! As were prepared decades ago, stored in jars. They're in a locker very far from here—too far for you to walk. Drop us a line, sometime, dear— "

"Yes, address it to 'The Misses Paul,'" said Marla, and the two women took up their things and left.

Standing alone on the vast roof which was now emptied of airplanes and noise, save for an echoing, windy sound high above, Dra— felt the familiar and strange, shadowy pain resurface in her back. Clucking to herself, she headed back to the toilet, the place where she would feel best right now, she decided, for the toilet's close wooden walls were dimly comforting, as was the idea of stubbornly sitting there for hours with no results.

Shutting herself inside the room, sitting, she sighed, pondering her problems with a silence like nails, far in the distance hearing a door bang shut. She imagined jumping up to race after Slim and Marla, and that upon hearing her approach, the two of them would turn and laugh gladly, welcoming her, saying that they had intended for her to join them for lunch all along, that it had just been a kind of oversight that they had forgotten to invite her, and that they would then exclaim with pleasure and take Dra— into their arms; and these thoughts were so compelling that she did, in fact, jump up, smooth her skirt, and run from the toilet after Slim and Marla, mouth watering at the thought of the tamales.

Winding softly down the stairwell, she glimpsed them a few floors below her, walking arm in arm. Perspiring, afraid to make herself known, Dra— trailed behind, taking care so they would not see her or hear her footfalls. Suddenly she had the distinct impression, as if from an objective, telegraphic source, that her future, though probably to include a good, dependable job, was certain to be brief and senseless.

Following Slim and Marla, she watched as they turned into a hallway then leaned toward one another in an ugly display of public affection. She raced ahead, hard prickles of anger on her scalp, not wanting to lose them, still hearing, almost in her bones, the vibrations of the indoor airplanes several floors above.

But she was not able to catch up; the two were distant now, difficult to see, and they passed through an enormous steel doorway at the end of the hall, which for some reason fell shut after them with a drastic, reverberating bang. Dra— sprinted toward the door, fearful that the Administrator would at this point likely banish her for her lateness, and finally reaching the door, she flung herself upon it with a sob. She tried to open it, though it had no handle, but suddenly it swung back from the other side, revealing a man in suspenders.

He stood opposite her, hands on curved hips, his hair consisting only of a few dark strands upon a bare, peeling scalp, although a strange, stiff, matted hair shadowed his forearms almost completely, with the likeness, disconcertingly, of a protective shell.

The man ushered her into a series of small rooms, speaking in a reprimanding tone that was in curious contradiction to his round, childlike face and rocking gait.

"That's a key, isn't it? It's not a good idea to walk around with a key ring, because first of all, it looks so sloppy," the man said, pointing to her skirt, where she kept pinned the small key to her old school gym locker, a souvenir kept from a single experience long ago.

"Most employees around here would never be seen with a key ring," he continued, still extending his finger. "I've heard some departments are lax in their rules and whatnot, but my thinking is, if you hold a set of keys, why walk around with them for the whole world to see? I don't like things seen," he concluded, glancing into the hall behind her and bristling.

She tried to move through the doorway, but the man stopped her with a large rubbery hand to her shoulder, and this angered her, but he smiled so ingratiatingly that she somehow wound up giving him a similar smile.

Shamefacedly, she explained that she wanted more than anything to find Slim and Marla, the two women she had recently met and just as suddenly lost, and that afterwards, she must find her Administrator, for whom she longed even more shamelessly, if that were possible; and then gasping with a cry—easily the loudest sound she had produced in months—she realized that she had made a terrible mistake and actually had missed the appointment with her new Administrator, that she had forgotten to go meet the woman at the train station as the Employment Manager had directed. And now, it was too late; sick in waves at the thought of this failure, uselessly puffing a hot stream of air from her mouth, the terrible finality of this error settled into her heart and she sank to the floor, raising her arms to her face, moaning softly, beyond tears.

"Don't you know anything about keys? A key should never be visible through the pocket," the man continued monotonously. "In my day, keys were kept by machinists, and we knew the worth of a key. We knew what badness was, and we knew that even pure nothingness exists right alongside everything else in the world, except we didn't make a big deal of it. Nowadays, there's so many mixed-up people who think they're fancy, tripping around the hallways talking about so-called new ideas and so forth, but most of them couldn't even lift a scrub brush if you asked them to." The man wiped his eyes, which were seeping, with a hand that shook slightly, not from emotion, it seemed, but from some sort of physical stress.

"Here's my question, Miss: how is it that you carry a key so late at night, when the men in charge of keys are all asleep?"

But Dra— was low against the doorframe, wiping tears, all disappointed emotions refracting and settling into a brackish mask across her face, for Slim and Marla would have walked far ahead by now, into any of many rivulet hallways where she would never find them, and worse, she would never find the Administrator, not at this point. As the man continued speaking, the grating below her feet, concealing an amassment of machinery, expelled a low, hollow whistle, and she pressed her mind toward a colorless horizon and managed to have no thoughts at all.

"You're coming to work with us, then, I suppose?" the man asked, turning around nervously. "We make our own grout here, and use it every day. We go slow. We don't stop working, and we don't talk about any wild ideas. We don't get fancy, and we don't hanker over the world as it might have been if people were different from what they are."

Looking at her, he gestured at the rooms around them and the long hallway leading away. "You'll see that when you work here, it's hard to imagine any other depart-ments exist at all. You stop being able to remember the other places you used to know, or if you do, you think they're dumb. Do you know why that happens? I sure don't."

The man helped her up, biting his tongue in between his lips in a gesture of distaste, then he led her into a musty adjacent room with empty shelves around its perimeter and a table of pastries in the corner.

"Here, Miss," he said, bending toward her hesitantly. "I see your lips are dry. Could I share some of this oil with you?" He offered a small container, leaning for-ward, eyes moving closely down the length of her body, then he slipped the container back in his pocket as if he had forgotten why he was holding it. She looked back at him, repelled by the closeness of his face, watching the sweat gather along his neck. Tears welled in his eyes, and as he spoke, he stepped even closer, pushing his face next to hers.

"To get something from another person, you've got to lose something, maybe everything," he whispered. "Isn't that what they say?"

"Is it?" she whispered back stiffly.

The man did not answer. Edgily, he tugged at the hair on his forearms. "Usually I don't think I'm mad, but if I feel I'm going toward an edge, an edge where you fall off and go mad, why, I take a pill, and the pill stops it from happening. Well, maybe a pill can also stop you from losing yourself to someone else. What do you say?"

"Well, yes . . . maybe."

"I used to wonder, Can the wind be stopped? No, I said, it can't, the wind comes from nature. But now I see I was wrong—nature can be stopped all over the place."

Drawing a breath, she waited, then said uneasily, "Nature doesn't care about us, does she?"

"Well, as a matter of fact, she doesn't," the man answered, smiling, leaning back with some relief. "No, nature doesn't care. She's a bad mother, and she only wants one thing from us."

"What is that?"

He gave forth a sniffing, suppressed laugh. "What in shit's name do you think?" He waited, then hesitantly reached forward, saying, "Can I just see inside your mouth for a moment, Miss?" and she complied, immediately tipping her jaw upward and opening it as the man said softly, "I want to see, that's all, just for a minute — I want to see if I was right about something," as he grasped the back of her head and shoulders.

Slowly he lowered her body to the floor, kneeling and peering into the mouth for some time. Then the man turned away, shaking his head violently and gripping his hands together for some moments, as if struggling with something he loathed.

The man stood, pacing around the room, wiping his brow. "It's strange getting to know someone, isn't it? Learning all the bad-smelling things about them — I don't care for it. I don't like new friends. I'm not partial to compliments, either, they don't agree with me; even when I hear the phrase 'you're pretty nice!' I'm at the edge of not wanting to live anymore. I'd wager you're the same."

Lying there stiffly, looking at him from the floor, Dra— lifted her head slightly and said only that she meant no offense, but she must leave immediately to go find her new Administrator, since the woman might be searching for her at this very moment, unable to find her because she, Dra—, was lying here on the floor of a half-deserted worksite, and that thought was too difficult to bear.

The man responded coolly, "Oh, you don't surprise me at all. I wasn't going to let you stay, anyway! I can see who you are, pretty much, and it reasons that lots of things about you are going to disagree with me in an awful bad way . . . in other words, there are lines I won't cross, Miss — and you seem to conjure up most of them." He looked to the floor. "Maybe most people do."

He moved to the doorway, blocking it for a moment with his girth. "Everything is wrong with everybody," he said to himself, going into a dark mail room nearby. From there he disappeared into a warren of smaller offices beyond, and, waiting there on the floor, worried about the Administrator and other things besides, Dra— looked down the length of her body and noticed a raw, sore bump shaped like a nipple on her upper arm, which began to throb painfully as soon as she perceived it. Then her entire arm and torso felt sore, and unable to think about this or anything else, she turned over and slept.

When she woke, the room was pitch-black, and immediately she called out for the man, who did not answer. Aching, she sat up, feeling a waxy piece of paper stapled to her skirt. Wending through the mail room and into the lighted hallway, she saw it was a note, and tore it from her. It was written by the man, and said she must stay and complete a task in this department in order to pay him for the frustration she had caused him, and also to test her skills, just in case one day he might be able to tolerate more in life, and so could call upon her to work with him. The task would not be too arduous, the note read, and after she had completed it, she was to go on her way. She was to work alone, it said, because the man could not bear to be in the vicinity during any part of this.

The note then listed directions for the job, which consisted of sending some old metal film canisters through a pneumatic tube system that was large as a city and also very old; the note added that Dra— must finish the work by evening's end. Glancing down, she found a second note stapled to her skirt, in which the man explained that he was worried about his son, who was growing rapidly day by day. This disturbed the man; he did not want his son to exist anymore, the note said, because the child was getting too old and complex, and too full of opinions. But the son would probably live, the man conceded; still, for his own comfort, the man would try to flatten the boy's personal dimensions, and for the time being, the man had gone away to find water.

Pondering the curious messages, she wandered into the empty workrooms, pleased at least that there was work for her to do; and it seemed peculiar that the task had come to her so easily, without her even asking for it, whereas in the Employment Office, the very center for job-hiring, it had taken considerably longer to procure work.

On a table before her, she found the canisters. Gathering them in her arms, she carried them to the tube, ready to push them one at a time into the slot. But the slot was locked, somehow; and when she found a key on the wall to unlock it, the key only opened the door an inch or so. It seemed that another key was needed at this point, or that the slot was jammed; but she reasoned she might simply remove the film from each canister and slip them alone into the opening, without the canisters. She would not worry about ruining the old film, she told herself, prying open the first canister with her nails, because the workroom was rather dark, and besides, the film itself was covered by a plastic wrap that was dark—certainly dark enough to obscure most light, though not all degrees of light.

So she worked in this way, removing the film from all canisters. The job went smoothly, and she hummed, but after some time she scowled in displeasure that turned to rage, for a few feet behind her she glimpsed a supply counter where a bearded man sat, watching her and smiling with great mirth.

After she noticed him watching her, she set to work at a furious pace, tearing the moldy film packets from the canisters and shoving them into the tube. Some of the packets were too large to fit into the slot, however, so in frustration she slammed her palm upon the slot then ripped off the dark plastic that covered the film, which actually proved to be not film at all, she saw, but small wooden blocks with crude impressions of life gouged into their sides. These she tried to jam into the slot, but could not.

Turning again to glare at the clerk, who grinned further and nodded his head, she began to shove all sorts of broken glass, debris, and dust from the floor into the slot, grabbing anything that came to hand, and then she took the empty canisters, tearing their lids off, and crushed them with her hard shoes, submitting the flattened pieces into the slot, spitting as she heaved an exhausted breath and slid to the floor where the man could not see. Panting, she saw lying on the floor a torn circular that had been enclosed with the film, warning of dire contaminants in the film.

Printed tightly together, some of the words on the circular appeared to be whole lines long, describing the many ways contaminants could enter the body, especially through the hands, for covering every human hand, it read, there were ten thousand tiny, spongy, eyelike openings which drank in poison readily, and there was nothing to be done about this fact but accept it grimly.

It was now very late, and as she thought of the Nurse once again, her innards contracted uncomfortably with unwanted, scarcely recognized wishes and her thoughts drifted to a time years before when a frightened, strong-smelling teaching assistant, Glisa, lips tacky with saliva, had made a confession to the class: "I didn't know him at all. We were talking about hobbies, not much more than that, and the next thing I knew, we were kissing! But that's how relationships begin, isn't it—with kissing? How else would they begin?" Dra— did not clearly hear what Glisa said next, though it had to do with blood pressure dangers, for Glisa's confession had filled her with a repulsion she did not understand, and she went to the class cloakroom to recover. There, she began to revive, breathing slowly and guardedly, for the air in the school had never been good, being full of chalk grains and throat-singeing airplane exhaust.

And now, she rose to leave the worksite, which was littered with the dark crumpled paper and the dozen or so smashed glass bottles she had hurled against the cement floor just because she had wanted to dispose of them and couldn't manage to do so properly. Passing the supply counter, she glanced at the bearded man, who was now eating from a bowl of mush, then fled the workroom, swearing to find the Nurse and also her Administrator, who surely, despite everything, must be close at hand.

Much later, walking along a bank of dark, unoccupied offices, she bent to retrieve a dusty handbill from the floor, which bore the names of some lower managers who recently had failed an important project and were being disciplined in a way that was not evident right now, but would be in years to come. Breath coming quickly, she scanned the names but did not see her Administrator's among them; flipping the page over, she searched, and finally saw it, deep within an article about ammonia and grain. And the very sound of the name and its syllables sent her heart lunging and plummeting; thrilled, clutching the torn paper, she ran wildly through the hall, possibly as excited as she ever had been, emitting a single hoot of excitement before quickly covering her mouth.

Rounding a corner, wishing to find a telephone, she saw instead a metal-green elevator which, as a sign indicated, roamed variously through all of space, seeking to pick up new employees and hurtle them to far-flung worksites. This elevator, she knew, was well known and fast as a train; though it always deposited passengers safely on firm ground and had never yet crashed, the risk of crashing was omnipresent.

Nervously, she steered away from the elevator, hoping for a safer way to reach the pump site. A short distance to her left, she noticed a single narrow doorway at the base of a sheer wall, shrouded in a kind of steam. Moving closer, she made out a faded sign above the door advertising a chiropractic. Peering in, she saw a stout secretary in a chair behind a typewriter, wearing a sleeveless blouse.

Encouraged greatly by this sight, Dra— entered the office and abruptly asked the secretary where the pump site and the new Administrator could be found.

The secretary, turning in her chair, replied evenly,

"This entire building is likely vacant. I'm the only one here—that's fine by me. I like it because I get so much done! Don't ask me where everyone has gone. Oh, I believe there's a man upstairs, but beyond that, no one's here. Would your Administrator be that man? Generally, he carries a poker. Everyone loves him dearly. If that man isn't your Administrator, I can't help you."

"My Administrator is not a man," she replied with great hostility. The secretary stared, folded her hands, then said, "Let me tell you a story," and proceeded with a quick fable about a bland young girl who once needed, in no uncertain terms, intimate guidance from an older woman and never received it, though once the needful period had passed, the girl did receive it, albeit in dreadful proportions.

At the story's end, Dra— wept for a moment then said, "I want to settle everything and begin working! I have to find my Administrator—"

"You haven't yet worked?" the secretary asked with incredulity; and recalling the film canister task, Dra— glumly realized it had been a rather unofficial job, so she could not count it as part of her work history, despite the frustration it had caused her and the odd sense of dissolution that filled her after its completion.

She sighed briefly. "Once I find my Administrator, all of this will be over. I'm so exhausted my head hurts and I think I may become sick!"

"Of course you'll get sick," the secretary quipped, stowing a set of thimbles in a drawer. "Everyone does, from germs that come clamoring out of nowhere to drag us into death!" She scratched her nose. "Aren't illnesses just a showcase for little creatures who are smarter and more sophisticated than we are, anyway?"

Dra— did not speak, and the secretary, eyeing her, asked again, "You don't have a job to go to?"

"No."

"Why not, in the name of living hell?"

By way of replying, Dra— gave a halting, obtuse account of her last brief meeting with the Nurse, which had been years ago and had taken place behind a cabin; then she cried, "I can't go to work without help; my Administrator will come, won't she? Otherwise, how will I get along?"

The secretary gave a great honking laugh. "You mean to tell me you can't go to work without your Administrator taking you there by the hand like a little pet monkey she's about to cane?"

"I don't know—" she answered, face blazing, ashamed.

"Don't tell me, honey," the woman said, waving her fingers. "This is all very sad. You haven't yet reported to work? But that's not good for your health! What have you been doing with your time? Now, I'll admit there's a frightening side to administrators, and depending on them is awful and not easy to describe, but still."

Hoarsely, Dra— managed, "But I failed—I missed our appointment! I wasn't at the station on time."

"Oh, she wouldn't have been there anyway, I promise you that," the secretary said. "Sit down and take some of this water, dear," she added with kindness.

The secretary reached into the desk to retrieve a soft metal cup, its side imprinted with the name of a nation long gone, and Dra—, sitting, emitted a shaky sigh.

"Headaches—of course you would have headaches, everyone knows these are caused by the people we know, or once knew." The secretary handed over the cup, filled with gray water, along with a second, larger cup that contained a familiar, turgid white liquid traditionally meant to encourage a bowel movement, though it was also said to calm the nerves while at the same time increasing thirst agonizingly.

Arms crossed, the secretary watched as Dra— drank everything down. Bringing the second cup to her lips—a moment before squeezing her eyes shut in revulsion and pouring the substance inside her—she noticed a small telephone attached to the wall; and as she finished the drink, gagging, replacing the empty cup on the table as the secretary swiped it away, she again directed her glance to the phone, burning to reach it. With a telephone, she could call not only the Administrator, but the Nurse. And if she was unable to reach either of them, she could just dial an operator who might locate them or give an explanation for their unreachability, or at least explain the strange, swarming thoughts this unreachability seemed to stir within her.

So, staring at the phone, Dra— began to weep with desire to use it, and also with the fear of asking permission for it; nevertheless, she resolved to ask, propelled both by urgency and the fundamental human need to make a successful telephone connection—the latter being something she had accomplished so few times in life.

The secretary, squinting, smiling, muttering, had now set an array of cups on the table, each smaller than the last, and was cleaning them one by one with a rag. Gesturing for her attention, Dra— silently indicated the phone and its shiny metallic receiver, no bigger than a hook, really. She cried more noisily, chiefly as a contrivance to gain permission to use the phone, but she also cried because she was genuinely shaken, she realized—by her terrible lateness for work, by not finding her Administrator, and by the disorienting, tiny shape of the phone.

"What the hell is the matter?" said the secretary, setting a cup down, stepping closer, unsteady on her high wooden shoes.

Dra— cried on, mouth open and inarticulate, before she managed a single watery sentence about the Nurse, and consolation, and the odd, sinking finality of meeting someone for the first time.

The secretary reached for the eyeglasses on a cord around her neck, staring archly. "Your problem is that you don't keep busy enough. You don't have interests. Haven't I got my little white figurines? Having interests whiles away the time.

"If you want to find your Administrator, that's fine, but get started with life, too. Oh, you could focus on your own feelings—so selfishly, as in those awful old radio songs—or you can move to the beat of time, finishing each day's business as nice as you please, finding job satisfaction and being content to know that anyone who achieves less than you will be ground down to less than nothing!"

Daunted, she grinned meagerly at the secretary.

"Why do you smile at me?" the secretary said. "Smiling is for dogs. In ancient times, it signified deference amongst them. Well, things haven't changed much, have they?" She smirked and went on: "Why must you see this nurse? Can't it wait? Do you have stomach troubles?"

"Maybe that's what it is."

"Do you have to go to the hospital?"

"Why, yes, maybe," she replied, though she had not considered it before; however, the idea sounded appealing.

"Oh, you don't want a hospital," the secretary said. "Because once I was in a hospital—do you know what it's like being set into a strange bed? Even if you're lucky enough to have a visitor, you can't kiss or hold each other or even cry together without the whole world walking by and a nurse walking in and sticking a thermometer in somebody's mouth."

Scarcely listening, unable to wait another moment, Dra— sprang for the phone, shaking, taking it by its curious metal loops while glancing fearfully at the secretary, who seemed not to mind this behavior at all, but only glanced down at her hands, as if considering a different set of troubles altogether.

Presently, though, she stood and reached out absently to help install the telephone's loops over Dra—'s fingers, murmuring, "There we are," and activating the phone by squeezing its center, hard.

The telephone emitted several simultaneous tones, and listening to these, trying to separate them in her mind, Dra— heard the secretary behind her explaining with a sudden burst of enthusiasm that this type of phone was very popular now, and that lately, it had caused quite a sensation in general because it had been designed with the idea that the phone and the user's mind functioned in identical ways, and soon the phone went dead.

The secretary said, "I see that look on your face, that

overly needy look that says all you want is someone to take care of you! That's trouble all over. People don't like that, you see. Oh, I know your type and the tricks you play. You'll cling like cream to try and find someone, anyone, to stay with you, and there's never an end to it, because you can't let go. I know your type."

"That's not true!"

"It's a crime, that's what it is. Funny, I could almost fall for something like that—when I was younger I did, you know, and nearly died from it too. Dependence, that's what we've been talking about all along—leaning on someone and leaking all your troubles right into their arms—is that any good? I'll bet this isn't the first time you've wandered the halls like some little addict, looking for the odd bit of kindness here and there. My question is, why do you do this? Are the causes chemical? There's got to be a reason!" The secretary turned in her seat.

She removed her glasses and sighed, pressing her eyes with her fingers. "Oh, sit down, why don't you?" she said to Dra— tiredly. "Shut your eyes; I'll get you something more to drink." She stepped away then returned not with the previous cups, but with a glass jar full of a heavy, sweet tea that Dra— immediately swallowed, its oily taste somehow eliciting a sensation of grief, and in turn, the tea seemed sadly to grow even sweeter.

The secretary sat next to her again, sighing, resting her head on Dra—'s shoulder as Dra— felt her face open with the tea's strange melancholy and her hand, heavy with the phone apparatus, fell to her side.

"Why, look, Missy, you've had no real help in your life, have you?" the secretary said, facing her, voice vibrating close to Dra—'s face, lips fleshy and pink. "A fool could see that every pore of your being is just begging for attention! Now, I'm not interested in this great big hee-hoo over your lost Administrator and the Nurse and what have you, with you roaming all over creation, searching for places that aren't even on the map. But I guess I understand. You just haven't found your niche in life. Everyone has a niche; what's yours? That's right," she said tenderly, reaching to pull Dra— onto her lap and against her breast.

In the long silence that followed with the secretary's hand pressing on her shoulder, Dra— began to weep again, the arid scent of her own breath coming back to her.

After a time the secretary shifted and said, "I just hate the qualities of a child in a grown woman, don't you? I hate a whining voice; I hate a lip blister. Well, everyone has their tics, I suppose. Take me, for example. I'm a giggler. Oh," she said, prying the phone's metal loops from Dra—'s fingers, "never mind this silly thing; it never worked anyway; you dial a number and it turns into an altogether different number, huge, growing always bigger, right into infinity before your eyes like a pestilence! I hate this phone." She threw the apparatus on the desk, producing an enormous crash, then smacked her lips contentedly.

"It's a problem to be so all alone like you are, I'll say," the secretary continued. "It's unfortunate. Now, listen to me. I'm going to tell you how to fix everything. Forget that Administrator—she's no good, none of them are. Why don't you get into a different boat altogether?"

"What do you mean?" she asked, her face still pressed

against the secretary's blouse.

"Well, do you know that long ago, when I began working, there was no one else here at all? I worked in solitary. But one day, a great many new employees came, there were so many, really, people were everywhere, all working away like fleas, yes, and how we talked! Actually, we didn't talk much in the least. Still, 'friends,' it's called, and it's not half bad! I'll have no truck with this mooning over lost administrators, you see, because there are always friends in this world. I had tons of friends, and after a while, do you know what happened? Poof!" She laughed unpleasantly so that lines of strain appeared across her face and disappeared in a moment. "They were all gone, every last one of them, because they were nuts. It happens like that in life. Just imagine: in the future, the friends you know now will be gone. We lose our friends over and over, many times, don't we? My!" the secretary sighed, smiling fondly, removing her glasses and wiping her eyes; and Dra— suddenly realized that they had not introduced themselves to one another.

"The world is so big," the woman murmured. "I wonder what would it be like to live so long that you could see the whole world change? And all its people, and all its parts, everything becoming so different, do you think that will happen?"

"Yes, I think maybe . . . yes, it will."

The secretary shifted. "Sometimes we need someone older, don't we?" And Dra— heard the woman's eyes click open and shut and felt the cool draft of her breath as they sat together uncomfortably on the office chair, rocking slightly.

"I've wondered how people fit together, and speak, and stay together," Dra— murmured.

"Oh? I know just what you mean!" said the secretary.

"You do? How does it work, then—how do people stay with one another so easily and talk for such a long time, as if it were nothing?"

"Oh. Well, if that's what you're saying, then I'm afraid I don't know what you mean at all."

"I mean, people staying together, days and nights of it—how do they do that, without scaring away?"

"Oh, Missy, that's the stuff of the world. Everybody talks to everyone else—they talk, and they get married; then they go to work, and by then life is nearly over, isn't it? People work, they drink water. They advance on the job." The woman shrugged.

"But what do they talk about? What things do they say?"

"Oh, anything, dammit, anything at all, what does it matter? Something funny, or something spooky—people just talk, don't they?"

"Talk about what?"

"Well, we're talking right now, aren't we?"

"Well, yes. You mean people ask one another for guidance?"

"Well, sure, they can do that."

"I've heard people speaking in foreign phrases I don't understand! I've seen things that don't make sense, that don't fit in with the rest—how can I—"

"Just forget anything like that, Missy, and concentrate on your plan for life. Why, you already have a job, so, at least in my book, you're ahead of the game."

"Well—I'll have to find my Administrator and get settled; then—"

"Oh, quiet," the secretary said.

"But, I'm lost, don't you remember?"

"Shut up, girl."

"If I hadn't forgotten to go meet my Administrator—"

The secretary broke away, now bent nearly to the floor in laughter, gasping, "Oh, you are funny! Missy, get to work, that's all! Gee, with your yipping on—get busy and don't bother with much else, that's my motto. Go on! And here's another piece of advice: If you don't understand directions, just ask! For example, if you got lost at a bazaar, wouldn't you ask how to find your way home? Well, if you don't understand the work assigned to you, just ask! Learn to ask!"

She stood and strode away, looking back at Dra—, shaking her bare arm, saying, "You don't ask, that's your problem. Yes, I know we all have difficulties in life that aren't our own doing. But we must take control of it all, in spite of that! Oh, you've got to ask," she sighed, wiping her eyes again.

For causing the secretary such strained emotions, Dra— felt remorse; nevertheless, she asked searchingly, "Are you talking about a kind of code for living?"

"Oh, be quiet," the secretary said, leaving the room for the adjacent kitchenette, calling from there, "I'm not your Administrator, am I? That's a question for her. It's a big question. By the way, did you know that most people in charge are self-hating? It's true." Her voice faded as she disappeared into the interior of the offices. "Everything's trouble, anyway," she was saying.

After a few minutes she returned with a bowl of silty water, slurping it greedily, gasping between swallows, "If you have an Administrator, she'll find you sooner or later, and if you don't find her, she's probably dead and you'll be assigned another. Why make faces over it?"

Later, exhausted, far from the secretary, though their conversation still rang in her mind, Dra— lay among a pile of rotted, overturned tables at an abandoned worksite with a ceiling so low that it was difficult to stand. She had not reported to the pump site at all, and though dreadfully anxious to do so, she was also loath to move at all, since her head rang with the same headache she had had for quite a long time. However, she vowed that from now on, all her energies must be spent in pursuit of reporting to work, and she wondered idly when she might find a train that traveled to the pump site. Chewing thoughtfully upon some rolled pieces of paper, downing water from her cup, she turned to a directory of toxins that lay on her lap, beginning to read assiduously. She had come across the book beneath some rubble nearby, and though the print was dark and difficult to make out, she grew deeply absorbed in the text, forgetting herself and her lateness.

After some hours she looked up from the pages, recalling the secretary who, waving tiredly from the doorway of the desolate chiropractic, called out that it would be wise to study and memorize books such as these, and also books that evaluated the chemical sources of not only pleasure and pain, but more neutral emotions as well.

And soon, she imagined, she would be sitting not alone but among others, working hard and in close proximity to her new Administrator, too. Upon arrival at the pump site, she would begin to work immediately, even before she was told what to do; though when life had settled into a routine, she considered, she indeed would probably search casually for a worksite telephone just to call the Nurse and chat over nothing at all. This tack would be much preferable to calling the Nurse in the middle of the night with profound anxiety or terror, which had occurred before, and which caused the Nurse to lose her temper.

So with a strong, even will, Dra— rose and wiped her hands, laughing suddenly, uncharacteristically, and with deep amusement as she realized that she had forgotten entirely about the Administrator for the few moments she had been pondering the Nurse. Humming, feeling a light, modulated emotion much like hope, she began organizing stacks of blank papers on a legless, battered desk, just to keep herself in form, and swept dust from the ceiling; then she set out to find the train that would lead her to the new worksite and new vistas.

After several hours, having found the way to the station on a wall map, she approached the place through the expansive Employee Tunnel, and caught her breath at the sight of the train itself, so intricately decorated with misshapen metal spires, coils, and a two-dimensional staircase. False windows above its passengers' seats were flung open so wide they seemed to be begging. She had heard this was a dependable train, speedy compared to other trains, and every day it ferried huge numbers of new employees to their worksites, albeit through an arduous system of uphill tunnels that caused significant delays. After crawling painstakingly through these, the train would finally arrive at its destinations, overheated; yet, Dra— had heard, new employees were actually well-rested and healthier for having ridden this train, and thus better able, at least for a while, to fend off illness as they began their new jobs.

So in the empty, echoing, high-domed station, she grew excited, thinking not only of the luck this train might bring, but of the joy she would feel when she rode it in the future—on visits to the Nurse, of course. But now, in the station, it seemed the train was not ready to leave, but instead stood quiet and intractable. Its first car bore a wooden placard that read "San Francisco," a destination she did not really comprehend, though small print on the placard described the place as sad and far away, a dumping-ground for old machinery and even lost employees who were transported there by train.

She stepped into the car and sat on a bench, thoughts still on the Nurse, and she began to plan, as before, the complex visit with the woman that would ensue after she, Dra—, settled into the new job. This visit would be different from all other visits, she conceded to herself: arriving on a train would be dramatic. And fully absorbed by the thought of stepping from the train and into the Nurse's arms, she realized how such a visit, lengthy and absorbing, would work to bring the two of them much closer than ever before. But she was unable to imagine that specific scenario, so in discomfort raised her purse to her face, holding it there.

She began to wonder if she should delay her trip to the pump site just a bit longer and run right now to find a train that would speed directly to the Nurse's compound, so she and the Nurse might have a single, though rushed visit. The brevity of such a visit would create intensity and urgency, and from the dark confines of this point, Dra— would be able to say all sorts of unimaginable things to the Nurse, lush, formless words that would emanate from her so easily and in such great numbers because they would be true, and because she would utter them not now, but in the future.

She might also tell the Nurse of the back-ache, and of other symptoms, too, including her nagging dreams of thin excrement trails, and listening, the Nurse's face would grow furrowed with concern, whereupon the two of them would exchange significant glances and the afternoon would lapse; and after that single perfect moment, Dra— would touch her own face as lightly as if the skin were water or the Nurse's own face, then without a word she would rise and leave the room, possessing enough strength to head for the pump site, the place she must go to begin the new life she was so anxious to begin.

Stopping first to visit the Nurse might make this long journey bearable, Dra— contemplated, sitting there in the quiet row of seats, yet she was unable to get up and leave. She longed for the train to rock into motion, because that might disperse the suffocating stench of the car, which consisted of petroleum and, it seemed, egg.

She looked up in surprise to see a matronly conductor in a uniform strolling down the aisle of the train, chewing on something dark, perhaps a meat stick. Smiling to herself, the conductor took a seat on the bench opposite, legs spread, elbows on knees, and, chewing, swallowing, asked openly, "Why are you on this train?"

Looking away, Dra— stated wearily that her primary destination was the pump site, yet under the conductor's arch stare, she finally added with discomfort that she did not want to go to the pump site at all, despite the fact that it would mark the beginnings of a lengthy and fruitful career. The truth, she stated monotonically, was that she had wanted, deeply, only, and for so long to visit the Nurse, nothing more, due to lonesomeness, and that this lonesomeness functioned like a vise to keep her tied to the Nurse in a pitiful way, and from this there was no respite.

The conductor removed a bottle from her pocket and squeezed a thick daub of lotion into her palm. "So, you are predisposed to feeling blue. What of it? Blue is not the worst thing," she said, calmly rolling the lotion between her hands until it thickened into the shape of a stick; this she set gently against the wall of the train car and continued her thoughts. "My question is, why do you want to see this Nurse before reporting to work?"

Dreamily staring out the window, Dra— recounted the spidery, shadowy ache far inside her back, and how it shifted like a man's voice inside her and made her notice her own body in unpleasant, unprecedented ways; it made her insignificant, she further revealed, and it required attention from the Nurse. All was worrisome, she added, rushing to complete these sentences, though afterward she fell silent before the staring conductor as again her mind flooded in torrents back to the Nurse.

"A back-ache is not so outrageous," the conductor answered flatly. "We've only been standing upright for two million years—and that's not terribly long, is it? Now, what is this ache really about? Could it be about, say, fears? You want relief from life's fears and uncertainties, I think. That is babyish."

Staring blankly past the conductor, Dra— said that in addition to the back-ache, she sometimes heard intermittent whistling sounds that seemed to come from the very bones of her body, sounds that possessed an urgency quite distinct from her own. Though she fought not to hear the whistling, she had heard it often lately, and it actually had the musical properties of many tiny, diamond-like melodies. The sound was difficult to quiet down once it began, she explained, though usually she managed to dispel for a while with sleep or, at least once, with a laxative. She had not heard the whistling for several weeks, she admitted to the conductor, but if it began again, it surely would require frank professional care, possibly surgery. If she tried to describe the whistling to the Nurse over the phone, she told the conductor, the Nurse might laugh in disbelief; so for sheerly practical reasons, Dra— did not want the whistling to disappear altogether, at least not until the Nurse could hear it too.

The conductor stared, and pulling lint from her dark-blue trouser leg said, "Let me tell you something. We think we understand our bodies but we do not. Every day of our lives we feel sensations that we will never understand. This is true for the brain too—that is, we think we have clear memories, but we don't. Memories aren't true! They're made-up pictures that help make our lives like a story. And the sensations in our bodies, well, those are little ruses, you see. Oh, I think it's delightful! No one really knows what a body can do, or what it's ever doing."

"Some people know," she said.

"Maybe they do," the conductor said. "But that would be rare. And you—you can't even tolerate the thought of a little sore in the small of your back, can you!" She fixed a calm, steady stare upon Dra—. "Why don't you change? After all, when a person changes, the people around them change too, and then that person changes all the more. Wouldn't you like to be part of something like that?"

"But how?" she answered sorrowfully, mind casting about emptily.

"Do you expect me to do everything for you? I'm not a machine! Though people seem to think I am," she said, smiling, shaking her head, and she stood. "Oh, I meet all sorts of people every day, right and left, and we have the most wonderful little chats like this. I can't imagine anyone not wanting that in life. Can you?"

She shook her head.

"Now, can you think of something pleasant to do with yourself while you wait for your Administrator?"

"Yes."

"Good," the conductor nodded in return, pulling a matchstick from her pocket, chewing on it. "Fret no more. Go home, fry an egg, climb into bed and think pleasant thoughts. This train is not traveling where you think, anyway; it will run into the mountains, which are frozen tonight. There we will stop to fetch a cache of beef and won't arrive at your Nurse's compound for several days, if at all. On the way, the train will fly so high off the ground it would probably upset someone like you. Your worksite—that's the place you need to go. I'm not much older than you, am I? But I carry myself as if I were older," the conductor remarked and left, tossing the matchstick over her shoulder.

Heaving a great, blowing breath of disappointment, Dra— stepped heavily from the train, purse hanging from her hand, and passed through the high-domed, empty station. She first despaired of seeing the Nurse any time soon, then realized there would be nothing wrong with finding a phone at any time, even now, and calling her—not to make an appointment, of course, but just to say hello, and, possibly, at the outside, to discuss some light personal matters. And if the phone call actually went well, she thought, it might mean that she could ask the Nurse to come pick her up in an airplane and take her away.

Gritting her teeth, bent on making the call this time without backing down, she pushed toward the main hallway and past a stair landing, startled to see a lone, thin boy lying face up who was clearly experiencing pleasure. Disturbed, she ran from the station, its domed ceiling and railed balconies behind her.

She pressed on, searching for a phone, quite far afield, she realized, and presently she slid into a series of hallways that worked to calm her, for cool air blew through them, along with the faint scent of solvent. The unmarked passageways were so deserted and bare that it was difficult to see distinctly or gauge distances; and she was mildly surprised to make out, at some point in front of her, a lanky, bony woman strolling barefoot with a quiet-looking man clinging to her arm. At once, Dra— headed toward them. The woman wore a shiny, rustling hostess gown and had an arm around the wiry man, who held a burning cigarette in his mouth. The man wore a paper robe, and as the woman rubbed his shoulder companionably, she laughed loudly, as if trying to dispel some disturbance clinging to them both.

Instantly Dra— followed them through the hall, lined along its ceiling with unending rows of black pipes which rumbled inside, expelling heat and cold. Moving closer, her eyes lingered on the couple and their unusually expressive faces, and also on the man's brief wrapper, which, she noticed, scarcely covered his thighs. Below his collar there was a rectangular patch where a name might be stitched, though it was not his name on the patch but instead, it seemed, a number to call in case of an emergency. And she considered that he might be ill, though his hair was thick and his color high, perhaps excessively high. The man and woman began to rub and lick one another avidly, as if preparing to have an experience, and at this moment, trembling with jealousy and anger, she approached them, crying, "Stop it, stop!"

Looking up, they eyed her with calm and stupor, leaning back upon the wall as one. With a soft whine, Dra— stared, imagining that she might run to them wildly, all reason lost, embracing them both with a madness that would surpass their voracity for one another, so that they would smile at her with contented, approving joy. And with tears over all the time the three of them had lost, the man and woman would then propose the obvious: that

Dra— join them in a permanent fashion so that from this evening forward, they all would be together, and Dra— would never return to her old way of life again.

But she could not run to the man and woman who stared blankly at her here in the bright hallway; they were strangers, after all. So instead she stared back at them steadily until they seemed to fade from her vision and likewise, they seemed not to see her anymore, resuming their kissing with vigor.

Presently the man turned away and began to roll a new cigarette, gumming it shut with his curling tongue. He leaned toward the woman, whispering something about the cafeteria, and eggs, and she laughed again, her face crumpling as if wounded by her laughter. She squeezed him around the middle, and he gave a mincing smile.

Watching these interactions, hearing the sound of their garments rustling together, Dra— experienced an onslaught of rage that filled her ears and caused her to clench her jaw and color, breathing hard. With surprise she noticed that the woman had seen this and now approached her, staring torpidly, saying, "What is it, baby?"

Face burning, she explained that she did not know what she wanted from life just now, not really, and though it would be nice to get to the bottom of things, that would probably not be possible, and so she must find her worksite, but at the moment everything was a bit too much. Though she wanted to find her Administrator very badly, she explained, what she wanted most of all was to sleep very soon, if sleep was even possible; and then she glared at the woman hostilely for having led her to speak in such a meandering manner.

The man giggled. Closing her eyes at the strong, sweet, fever-like scent emanating from the woman, Dra— suddenly turned to her, all irritation vanished, asking hopefully to know the woman's full name, explaining that simply having this knowledge would give her the anchor she desperately needed, and that it was something she might repeat to herself later, since she had no idea when she would find herself separated from them and alone again.

At least in knowing the name, Dra— also reasoned aloud, she would have a good chance of being able to recall the woman clearly in the future. Then leaning over slightly, hand flush upon the wall, she waited, certain that a denial of the request would set her back considerably with primitive grief.

But there was no stumbling-block, for the woman laughed openly and warmly, folded her hands across her rumpled gown, then compliantly stated her name, which turned out to be fantastic, ending with a flourish of lisps and pebbly syllables that Dra— found unpronounceable yet satisfying all the same. Looking up, shaking in sheer relief at the woman's immediate response, she gave forth a peal of laughter, and the man and woman laughed, too.

"Oh, we have such fun together, don't we?" the woman said, taking all their hands together, and in the giddiness of the moment, Dra— mentioned flirtingly that once, long ago, she had labored as a maid.

The woman waved her off, saying, "Sugar, you're over-tired, I can see that right away. Haven't you had anything to eat?" and she turned to deliver a long open kiss to the man, who had been tapping gently at her sleeve and now whimpered so protractedly with the kiss that he seemed to be in pain.

The woman fastened her eyes on the little man. "I can't stand the thought of him being away from my body, even for a moment, do you see what I mean? The real dream is to be attached to someone day and night, every moment of the year, without a second's interruption" she paused—

"—and when the pain of suffocation sets in, why, that would be just as dramatic in its way, I suppose." She kissed the man again, hard.

At the sticky sound of their kiss, Dra— began to sob with another burst of fury that jetted through her body; and, ears ringing, she faced the wall again, waving her hand to indicate they should turn away, though they were oblivious to this signal, and she sank to the floor, chest heaving. After some time she set her head against the wall, reaching out to touch the glimmering train of the woman's gown, and begged in whispers to know if the two were married.

"Of course we're married; what do you think this is?" the woman replied, smiling, looking sleepily down at Dra—, her warm, tanned arms opening. "Come here, baby, why do you hide in the wall?" She bent down, yawning widely, and the man put his face in her sleeve, rubbing it there.

"Attraction is just about the same thing as marriage, I think," the woman went on, smiling, mouth large and elastic. "The moment you're attracted to a person, isn't it all written? People pair off, that's all. Why, in the old days, we made love just as easily as we breathed, and soon enough we were set for life." She pulled close, nesting her chin in Dra—'s shoulder for a moment, digging it in. "Nowadays, people are scared to lift their eyes up to one another, aren't they?" She stepped back and laughed, shaking her head so her hair flew up. "Do you know what? I'm silly. I don't think he and I are married after all. I can't quite remember." She turned back to the man and held his head between her palms while he gripped her arm tightly, struggling against the pressure, not seeming to hear her. "I always forget what is and what isn't, don't I?" the woman said. "Let's see. I thought we were married because in my mind I have always been married and part of things, but the truth is I don't quite know! Maybe we forgot to marry, or, maybe we couldn't tell the difference between can and can't?" She looked at the man, grinning. "Maybe we planned a wedding, but I think we forgot about it, didn't we, Jann?" The man snickered.

"We could marry right now with no problem, if that's what you like," the woman went on, picking at her nails. She looked at Dra—. "You could be married with us—that's what you want, I can see. Well, why not? It'll be a marriage between Jann Farr and me, and you. What could be easier? It might even make Jann less low—he gets lonely and low, you see, and we don't know why. He gets bowel cramps and doesn't like to talk. He likes soup. Oh, he doesn't pay attention to very much in life—he just wants to be with me, is all. Isn't everyone always searching for a way to stay together? Sure, they are. I say we all get married, and afterwards, we'll take a nap."

Listening to the ongoing sound of the woman's voice, Dra— remained tightly against the wall, blinking, and the man, scraping a small curved hand along the woman's gown, whined for more attention. The woman turned to him and then the couple thumped together against the wall, exciting themselves as the woman called out breathlessly to Dra—, ". . . But I confess I'm not real good at friendships! I tend to drift," as Dra— began to cry again, this time with a gruesome sense of isolation which recalled, for some reason, a lecture she had attended many months before, on the eve of her acceptance into the employment pool.

It had been a special, formal evening, though she had been troubled by the odor of urine the entire time; no one had spoken to her, either, nor she to anyone—and that night, she had seen The Man with No Hair sitting in the row ahead of her, rigid and unblinking, the picture of paralysis. The speaker that evening, face and mouth covered almost entirely by bandages, was describing something he called "the shadow of self-cruelty," a difficult idea to explain, he shakily put forth, yet it grew even more imprecise when he tried to convey it with maxims. It could be best understood while lying face down, he finally said, and grew weepy over the subject, which was clearly close to him. The speaker reached for words and tried to take them apart for the purpose of giving the audience insight, but his speech grew absurd; and as he said the unfamiliar word "glickson," he spilled his mug of drinking water across his front, chilling himself. For the remainder of the lecture he had simply stood before the audience, teeth chattering, blinking back tears.

After some time the woman staggered over, pushing Dra— onto a heap of pillows on the floor, then fell down next to her, saying, "Why such a crybaby?" as she tied the sash of her gown. "You feel left out, I guess," she said, "but that's the kind of thing that makes me soar! I love being a little ahead of everyone. I love being married, and I love being smarter and luckier than others. Why don't we all go down to the storeroom, get married, then find some water to drink—aren't you thirsty? After marrying, you'll feel you belong to something, sugar." The man crept next to the woman and lay stiffly on his side.

The woman propped herself on her elbow and took the man's cigarette, smoking it, considering things.

"It'll be an easy marriage," she mused, "and anyone who says it isn't will be a fraud. Why, we could invite the skeptical to join in if they liked. Why not? I don't mind changes like that. I like things loose and easy. Shouldn't people be tied to one another in every possible way? Then we stand the least chance of having to roam around alone. It's true, I can feel it in my bones," the woman said blandly, sighing.

"Oh, silly, silly," muttered the man, mouth on the woman's shoulder.

Rolling over, stretching her arms, yawning and sitting up, the woman continued, "I've got Jann, at least. You can see we're never apart."

Quietly, Dra— began again to cry.

"Oh, you cry because you look at me and see how free a person can be!" the woman exclaimed, patting hard between the man's shoulder-blades, small as a doll's. "You feel constrained, you think your life is fixed in stone. Well, sugar, it's not! Listen to me. You can choose what you like to do, and when, and how. Isn't that what you want? We're all seeking little escapes, aren't we, one after the next? Well, go on! You pick your own path, your own instruments of justice, anything you please! Everyone does it."

"No they don't!" she cried.

"Ah, there's a loser for you," the woman remarked in a tired, easy-going way. She rubbed her lower gums for a moment with a finger. "Stay here with us, will you? I like you, and I like the way all this feels." She tamped her heavy, dusty bare foot on the floor.

"But, my Administrator—"

"Oh, blow it to hell!" cried the woman with irritation. "Forget that woman. You don't need her when you can come with us. If you play your cards right, you'll see that life is good and long, and nothing is as hard as you think."

"Do you mean that life is easy, but we just try to make it hard?"

"Well, yes, yes, that's it!" the woman looked at her in surprise, mouth smiling, open. "That's right." She smoothed her flimsy robe. "Let it all out, honey, say whatever you like."

Awkwardly, Dra— stared at her, pulling at a thread at the top of her skirt.

The woman went on gently, "I just don't believe in complicated problems, see. It's a trick I learned when I was a baby. You can learn it, too."

Nodding seriously, Dra— agreed, and she lay back, quietly beginning to describe for the woman a frequent daydream of hers in which she, Dra—, walked confidently, perhaps even with a trace of ennui, into a departmental bathroom, only to reemerge a few minutes later without a care in the world, then moved onward to the Nurse's outpost to wait for her, harboring none of the tension or despair of individuals who are routinely defeated by life.

Dra— omitted the last portion of the daydream, which involved meeting for regular discussions with the Nurse in a trailer, and she stowed this privately away so she might savor it later.

The woman looked at her curiously, loosening an earring. "Do you know a secret about me?" she asked. "Say no."

"No."

"That's right, you don't, and I'm going to tell you." She leaned forward, onto her palms. "No one is good enough for me. That's my feeling, down deep. I hate people just a little. Do you think that's bad? Well, it's part of me and I don't care!" She turned onto her stomach. "My little brother was so splendid that I was always called 'The Awful Giant,' but I never gave a hang and I still don't! I go my own way and keep relaxed. It's a talent most don't have. Nothing bothers me, and everyone is jealous of that!" She laughed, slapping the man, and he flinched. "I try to make them even more jealous so they'll appear ugly and then I can hate them less—but that doesn't always work." She sighed. "Aren't you jealous of Jann and me?"

"No."

"Yes you are, but no more than he is about you." The woman pinched the man on the neck, and he moaned and began to snuffle into her hand. "I'm the strong one, and that relaxes me so," the woman said, pulling him close.

Staring at the man and woman's hands fastening and twisting upon one another, Dra— felt her anger rise again and her will leak away; she curled against the coarse pillow, closing her eyes, groaning to the woman, "Please, let me find my Administrator!"

"Oh, listen to you!" The woman looked up. "What do you want from her? You're so sick over her that I'd just as soon bring her to you right now, but I'm too busy. Besides, she's no easy cup of tea, you know."

The woman stroked the man's head as if to shield him, and went on. "It's terrible, the way she never even bothers to come wave hello to a pretty girl like you and all the others! Forget it, that's what I say. Wasn't she supposed to come and take you under her wing? Well, she didn't. It's over now: don't brood."

Dra— lay back. "But I've heard that she is beautiful," she breathed.

"Maybe she is, maybe she isn't," the woman said. "You have a hard time with making decisions, don't you? I pity that." The woman lay back, then sang a few bars of an outmoded work song.

Presently she sat up and combed her hair vigorously for a few minutes. With a hand beneath the man's head, she cuddled him protectively as he stared upward, moving his lips scantly, as if reciting to himself.

"Mustn't I find her soon no matter what she has done? After all, she's my Administrator," Dra— said, then lay back, and presently, she felt herself dropping off to sleep.

"What is the best way to live?" the woman was muttering close to Dra—'s ear. "The newscasters say we should live well, and try to show us how, but we're not much up to that, are we? It's all like a dream, far away." They all dozed off for some minutes.

Dra— heard the man whining and opened her eyes.

He was petting the front of the woman's blouse, and the woman, waking, regarded him with a distant silence. Then she turned to Dra—, saying softly, shaking her head with disappointment, "Look at you, look at your skin, your neck, your hands, all ruined, ruined by worry," and Dra—, greatly burdened, fell back to sleep.

Much later she woke, and turning over, found herself face to face with the man, who rested along the length of the woman's body, a cigarette in his fingers, and his eyes, slitted, shone desperately with desire.

"How old are you?" she asked him in a whisper, but the man turned his face into the woman's breast.

The woman woke. "Why can't people do exactly what they like in this world?" she said loudly and plainly. "Doesn't time feel terrible when it's wasted? For God's sake, stop thinking about that Administrator! If I could, I'd reach into your head with a stick and poke all those thoughts out of you." Standing, she scooped the man into her arms and moved down the hall; then she turned, calling back somewhat ruefully, "I'll always remember your little body sleeping next to mine, so full of misgivings!" and with a sagacious air strode away while Dra—, still lying on the floor, called after them not to leave.

"Oh, sugar, you remind me of myself, exactly one decade ago," the woman called back to her. "I was just like you—strained, broken-hearted, all those things. I was quiet, just to avoid the arousal of men! Oh, I changed, and so will you. Suddenly I wanted a man, not in my heart, but in my stomach—that's how it happens, and no one knows why." She walked to the end of the hall, feet slapping loosely on the tile floor, then came upon an upright ladder leading, it seemed, either to the next floor or a storage compartment. Still carrying the man, she climbed it.

Lying exhaustedly among the tough-skinned pillows, Dra— contemplated with discomfort the silence left behind by the woman and man. Exhaling, squeezing her eyes shut, she suddenly recalled a day long ago when, fatigued beyond plausibility, wishing desperately for a job, so thirsty her pulse had pounded high in her dry eyes, she had stood near a moderately busy airstrip, watching small fleets of indoor airplanes taking off at intervals, ferrying huge numbers of employees to their worksites. The planes' old black bodies shuddered as they lifted off, rear engines pouring smoke and dripping with moisture. It was the moisture that tantalized her, she remembered, for she had needed water so badly on that day. She imagined running to one of the roaring planes, swinging herself atop its wing, grasping the propeller base and fixing her lips and tongue there and along its nub and inside its vents too, and everywhere upon the plane's body's hammered seams where the gassy, gritty condensation would be hers to lick up; she would beg for more, she imagined, and cry out from the relief and discomfort of drinking. Imagining it, she almost had been able to taste the moisture, which probably would have been satisfying and not immediately toxic; and she considered how drinking in spasmodic gulps from an airplane in such a fashion would really most closely resemble a homecoming—in fact, all that afternoon she had been full of the unmanageable desire and anger common to homecomings, emotions so bright and obtrusive that they both magnified and blotted away their source.

And recalling that afternoon's zestful imaginings, just as thirsty now, perhaps, though more accustomed to it, she also recalled the endless, borderless night before that afternoon at the airstrip—she had no longer been a schoolgirl then, but had not yet been admitted to the employment pool, either, so it had been the time in her life when she had been nearest to being absolutely nothing—a night when she had felt so quietly out of sorts: not abandoned, for there had been no one to abandon her, yet living in a prospectless twilight all the same. Standing in the overheated corner of a bare atrium, she had heard the faint sounds of flushings and laughter, and, after a moment, a hidden voice spluttering out angrily, "Sonofabitch!"

On that evening, she had spotted two tiny approaching figures, one of which, as they grew closer, she identified as Dr. Jack Billy—so old, in slippers, head down, speaking sadly and at great length to a child nurse who trod beside him, helping him walk. He looked as if he were making some kind of confession. As they approached, Dra—, half-hiding behind a buzzing air grille, heard the doctor weakly describe his failed attempts with the French horn, and also a medical examination from long ago that still upset him deeply. The child nurse carried a footstool at her waist.

The story of the examination was simple: when he had entered the exam room, there had been not one, but two quiet women on the metal table, one woman, the smaller, lying directly beneath the other. But to the doctor's regret, he had not realized the second woman had been there until days after the exam. During it, he ran his finger along the crevice where the two torsos met, absently wondering what sort of anomaly it was, thinking back to his training and finding a theory that, in its very concept, brutalized the patients. He derived subtle pleasure from the theory, though it provided no answers, and gently he applied some suction to the crease in hopes of solving the puzzle before him, but nothing happened. Disturbed, he finally looked down at the woman whose face he could see, and pronounced her unable to have children.

Recalling the incident, Dr. Billy cried, ashamed, for it called to mind similar incidents in which he had not dared question his training. He was more sad than Dra— could have imagined him—perhaps the single regret refracted into a larger, overarching grief—and he sobbed rhythmically, hiding his eyes, finally lowering himself onto the stool the child nurse placed before him. He admitted wetly to her that for years, his wife had not come close to him, nor had he wished her to, and that jars reminded him of conjugal life; and that lately, he had no yearnings for anything except to feel terrible. He said he wanted to open his mouth onto another mouth and inhale everything then choke on the lack of air, because the need to damage himself and others was consuming, as it had been all his life.

Slowly, the doctor grew calmer, more circumspect, and spoke of his profession.

"We set bones, though not often. We listen. We give pills without enthusiasm. There is a great deal of affection for patients that we must ignore. When patients ask, 'Why, underneath it all, do I feel so bad?' we give prescriptions, allow them to search the advertisements, read about magical treatments, and even formulate alternate codes for living, yet we never bother telling them: 'you have merely been infected by someone very close.'"

Remembering all this as she lay torpidly in the hallway, breathing, blinking into the crook of her arm, hearing the soughing sounds of a nearby air regulator, Dra— wondered where Dr. Billy had come from, and if he was even real; she wondered how she could have waited against the air grille all that strange afternoon, listening so intently, and watching out for something else which she desired vastly but would not recognize until she had seen it, though evidently, she had not seen it.

Now that day was gone, though she could still see the way the doctor hunched on the stool, hands hanging between his legs, and how he rose and walked away in nearly the same halting, abstracted manner as the small woman who at this moment was walking through the far end of the hallway, seeming to head straight toward her. And with an onrush of alarm Dra— sat up, knowing as if with instinct that it was her Administrator.

Floundering to her feet, Dra— fashioned a quick wave, feeling faint, gazing at the woman who was, after all, immeasurably important, and yet who, with her small frame and rather jerky gait, seemed to possess much less stature and prominence than expected. Approaching, the Administrator gave an awkward wave back. She wore moccasins, and draping her thinness was a light, limp dress so impossibly filled with flowers that Dra— began to cry.

As the Administrator arrived, she linked her hands with Dra—'s, holding the mass of their scaly red flesh near

her eyes and staring at it with consternation before fling-
ing it all down again and saying, "Hello! I am Mrs. Covers," then sneezing violently. Gawky, the woman moved
away, gesturing widely and tripping. As her thin fingers
moved through the air she looked at Dra—, adding, "And
it's a thrill to meet someone as tiny as I am!"

The Administrator's face, she noted, was kindly and
warm. On thin, flexing legs, the woman stepped toward
a door behind her as Dra— followed through the narrow
passage with its low ceiling and omnipresent hissing of
pipes.

The Administrator stopped. "Aren't you almost in-
sane for want of water? Most are. 'We like to find water
whenever we can,'" she sang abruptly in a small voice. "I
love that song, don't you? Of course we'll find water, you
can be sure." She stared for a moment. "You know never
to bathe in it, don't you?"

They entered another passageway with a staircase that
did not ascend or descend, but instead lay sideways on
the floor, so that, bent, they had to take intricate, picking
steps in order to pass over it.

It would be prudent, Dra— decided then, to take
this opportunity to inform the Administrator about her
work history and training, which, though meager, she
now began to say, was shored up by a well-tempered
yet ferocious desire to work regularly at any sort of
job, clerical or otherwise; and she added that though
she sometimes floated into a kind of paralysis while on
the job, she was generally competent, and could answer
telephones and use maps; she was also well-familiar with
record-keeping, owing to a grim daily diary of bowel

habits she had maintained for several years in a row.

The Administrator continued to lead the way through the hall. "Why is it that when people begin talking together, a thousand doors swing open and it's all so exciting and rich that one becomes lost and wants to die just from happiness?"

Dra— made no reply, though the Administrator continued without pause, "On the other hand, can we really be held accountable for everything we say or for the primitive nature of speech itself?" while patting her palms together rhythmically. "Oh, we'll talk anyway, won't we? We'll talk about longing and repletion and that hollow, withering feeling one gets when answering a telephone; or you could tell me about the food and eating problems you have; or why, for the life of you, you can't remember your mother."

Staring ahead through the dim, stuffy hall, groaning once to herself as they passed a pile of odorous, dark-soiled plastic sheeting, Dra— otherwise remained quiet, noticing, as she breathed, the faint sound of the whistling in her chest. She began to long painfully for the warm, lanky woman in the dressing gown and her man; and thinking sentimentally of the moments she had lain with them on the hallway floor, sunk in sleep, her eyes teared. She wanted to ask the Administrator's permission to retreat through the passageways to find them, but she could not remember their names, nor scarcely what they looked like, so her only recourse was to follow the Administrator and continue longing for them, which was actually steadying in its way, for the longing seemed both to whet and satiate itself.

The Administrator turned to face her. "Do you know this morning I saw a swallow?" the woman said and smiled, eyes crossed slightly in pleasure.

In silence they tracked through further spokelike hallways, possibly, Dra— began to hope, now rather hungry, toward the cafeteria with its rows of partitions and light bulbs suspended from the ceilings by cords. But as they drew nearer to the cafeteria, the Administrator walked straight past its entranceway which, in any case, was sealed by caulk.

Instead, they moved up a stair which fed into a room containing two chairs and small, high window through which a blackness like night's showed through.

The Administrator fell clumsily into a chair and smiled vaguely at Dra—, who began to sob with the long-unreleased tension of waiting for the woman who was at last here, and who was indeed different than others had let on, with her strange clothing and oily, flat hair. Lowering herself into a chair opposite the Administrator, placing her palms to her damp face, Dra— suddenly remembered that decades before, a bucket of sand had been upended on her head by another little girl.

In a few minutes the sobbing ebbed, and the Administrator leaned forward. "Let's talk," she said, as Dra— looked at the woman's feet, thin and set apart on the slanted floor.

Eyes still leaking, Dra— demanded suddenly, angrily, "Where have you been?" with seething tension and hostility.

"Where do you imagine I've been?" the Administrator said sweetly.

"I was supposed to meet you ages ago! You were supposed to train me for work. But I missed our appointment at the station—"

"You did?"

"—and it was all terrible, and now I have so many things to ask . . . and . . ." she panted in anger.

"What things?" the woman asked quizzically.

She waited, then answered mournfully, "Well, I don't know! It's about work. And about my difficulties."

"Difficulties? What difficulties?"

"Oh, I don't know! With needs," she managed.

"You have difficulties with needs?"

"Yes. And with feelings . . ."

"What on earth does that mean?" the Administrator asked.

"Well, I don't like them very much."

"Ah, my girl!"

Pleased with the attention the Administrator was paying her, she ran her fingers through her hair at the back of her skull, attempting to prettify it.

"Who enjoys those awful things we call 'needs,' or even feelings, for that matter?" the Administrator said, her face both smiling and a mass of worried lines. "Why, no one, really. Who can blame you?" She shifted a hip in her chair. "Let me tell you something. Most girls miss their administrators deeply in their hearts, do you know, even when that administrator is standing right beside them, leafing through a magazine. Girls so often grow sad, isn't it strange? But it's true."

Dra— sat up. "I didn't miss you deeply in my heart!"

"And girls frequently grow angry and ill with

headaches and—in your case—go to see Dr. Billy for treatments!"

"I didn't see Dr. Billy!"

"But you called him."

"I didn't!" she protested.

"You wanted the Nurse, you wanted the doctor. But, son of a gun, what you really needed was me!"

Staring at the floor, mind aswirl, she imagined herself breaking from this room as if from the top of a box and leaping onto the first fast-plowing train that passed, a train which would impel her in wild circles and at great speed to the Nurse and only the Nurse, or perhaps, in a chance beyond chance, into the lap of the very woman who sat before her; and imagining this, she cried out until her mouth burned with the simple, punishing taste of wishes.

Then, in the mirage-like silence that hung in the room, the Administrator, flushed, said quietly, "Isn't it strange that people possess strength, even when there is really no good reason that they should possess it?"

Dra— then broke into fresh, pestilential sobs, holding her elbows as if to comfort each, while the Administrator's voice rang out intensely, "You see? Female sadness is everywhere! Women are sadder, everyone knows that. We put women in groups and ask them to look at pictures of sad faces or of a war, for example, and they cry and cry, maybe from shame! Why shame? We don't know, or rather, we do, but we can't say it and expect anyone to listen! When people and animals are sad, they can't calculate well and their desires disappear and that's because sadness takes over the brain like you wouldn't believe." She gave forth a tempestuous sigh.

Dra— stared dumbly with a rattled, amazed expression at the woman, who grew quiet, her troubled, complicated gaze fanning across the room and settling onto a small apple that lay on the floor.

"Why not come along to luncheon with me in the Administrators' cafeteria?" she asked. "Solitary tables only, you know, but they move on an up-and-down course, spinning like wild things—it's exciting! Marvelous eggs. We'll talk and talk, for years if you like, about our relationship, and other people, and about the way bodies work; we'll talk and talk until there's nothing left but ashes all around us. Isn't that what a relationship is?"

"Ah—?" was her disbelieving reply, and as her eyes flickered toward the Administrator's with suspicion and appreciation, she became aware of a sensation inside her much like warmth. Motionless, she stared at the back wall of the room, which was covered by bundles of wiring.

Her agitation had evolved into a slow, rich, ravishing happiness which, though first seeming to emanate from the Administrator, was actually formed, she saw, of her own sprawling muscles and veins; as she lowered her head, the happiness revolved like an object, possessing organization and breath of its own, and she rolled her eyes to gaze at it, for it was like a long, complicated story, and she began to read it.

The Administrator, now winding a skein of gray yarn around her hands, was saying with quiet anxiety, "Isn't it strange, how people need one another? Some days, I tell you, I still can't believe it's true."

The woman rose and reached her arm into a drawer inside the wall, retrieving a small telephone, the sight of

which made Dra— close her eyes and inhale with rolling pleasure, for the instrument was made of smooth
glass that curved into dips and hollows just as alluring,
certainly, as was the heady promise of using it endlessly
and exclusively to call another party, someone who like
a miracle devoured and filled up everything in life in the
same effortless way that other people merely sat and
breathed.

Standing against the wall, the Administrator shook
and warmed the phone in her hands, trying to activate it;
then, succeeding, she placed it to her ear, as Dra— stared
dazedly at the woman's beige stockings.

And later, as the two of them walked past the mouth of
the dank Employee Tunnel, Dra— far behind the Administrator, she stared at the stockings still. As they rounded
the tunnel's final bulbous turn, entering the huge, damp,
greenish station with its walls coated by a whitish substance, it dawned on her that they had come here because
the Administrator was going to leave on a train, and
Dra— stumbled forward, aware of numerous uncomfortable physical symptoms she dared not communicate.

It was true: for the Administrator was now calling
wildly through the station for a train, and in between
these shouts, she described Frida, her young assistant,
who would be arriving soon.

"Frida is in nursing school," the Administrator explained, "so she has low self-esteem. Be tolerant of Frida,
won't you? Watch out for one another while I'm gone.

As for me, I have so many places to go, I'm dizzy! I do love rushing around, busy as I please; but don't worry, if there's a tornado warning I'll race back here to you, umbrella in tow!" She picked at a near-transparent eye tooth. "Do try to understand that it doesn't really matter if we can trust another human being or not—what matters is that we never feel we can.

"Oh, someday, you're going to spring to life, I can just feel it! Then you'll feel much less comfortable in the presence of pain," she added.

Without another word the Administrator stepped onto the low train that departed as instantly as it had arrived, curving silently along the thick walls of the station, which were meant to deaden sound.

And observing this Frida—who now bounded across the platform toward her in overwide, enthusiastic strides, clutching her notebook to her schooldress, dark frizzed hair tied back in a short ponytail, and whose tongue extended sinuously from her mouth nearly to touch her nose, and who, with overbearing, cheesy breath, Dra— uncomfortably imagined, would be garrulous and difficult to withstand—she realized unpleasantly that the Administrator had vanished, and that she, Dra—, was now utterly alone with a stranger.

Out of breath, perspiring, busty in her dirty uniform, Frida ran up, scratching at her ears and neck. "I'm glad you stayed, I wanted you to, but now that I see you, you seem almost unreal!" She panted with a frantic smile, rolling her eyes, taking hold of Dra—'s neck with a hand and squeezing for a moment as if to verify her presence. "Do you know that feeling of unreality?" Frida said. "I do.

I was afraid you wouldn't stay with me and that would have made me die, because that's what uncertainty does, it kills, sooner or later, that is. The Administrator said you might not want me along! But here you are. Doesn't everyone want a little company? Sure they do, even if they've studied theory in school for so long that they can't admit it."

Frida turned away, running, leading Dra— through the swinging, tar-soaked door of the station and into a hallway filled with hingeless, broken cabinets and the dismembered legs of office desks. "For heaps of reasons, I wanted you to be here," she went on. "I've always wanted a real friend and never had any, except for Pat Cook, but that was finished in one second. Please, won't you come to the bathroom with me?" Frida, very nearly begging, was still breathless; and at the touch of the girl's hand on her arm, Dra— agreed to go.

They moved through a steep downhill hallway and found at its end a deserted guard's station with doors on either side, each leading into the same enormous bathroom.

"All my life I've had to go to the bathroom alone and I hate it," Frida said bitterly, palm on the door. Her eyes filled with tears. "Why stay alone when it's so difficult? But 'no,' they say, and firm themselves against you." She cried for a moment, stopped, and then with great interest began to examine the surface of the nearby wall, fingering its texture, made up of small brown rises that appeared like human faces.

"I know something about the Administrator," Frida whispered, turning to look at Dra—. "She has a secret."

"She didn't tell me that," Dra— said.

"Of course not!" Frida yelled, flushing. "But it's true. There are other things that are true."

"What is?"

"I'll tell you, maybe," said Frida, pulling her face very close, a scent of paste surrounding her. "The Administrator loves the pleasure of sadness. Do you understand?"

"Not really."

"Well, I understand it quite well," Frida said assuredly. "She argued with Peter, and then she said to another Administrator, Miss Ulrich, that she was the most terrible mass of raw emotion, and that it all had to do with Miss Ulrich and Peter both and that it was unnatural."

"Who is Peter?" asked Dra— with distress.

"Then they talked about the pleasures of sadness, just as I expected they would," said Frida breezily. "It's all disturbing, do you see? Our Administrator wants us to long for her, that gives her the best pleasure. Do you know why?"

"No."

"Oh, I can't be bothered to explain it, but it has to do with conflicts by the dozen and never getting enough from loved ones." Frida sniffed. "Maybe sometimes at night she just gets so passionate about everything, about Peter and Miss Ulrich and her mother until she, you know, just explodes! That's how some people have fun," Frida finished dryly.

"Who is Peter?"

"Oh, nuts to you." Frida wrapped her arms around herself and closed her eyes. "People have all kinds of fun," she intoned mysteriously. "Someday, I'm going to write a book about our lives, and in it, I will talk about pining and pleasure—and electric motors, too."

"Maybe you won't write a book at all," Dra— said with sudden irritation.

"I will! If I say I will, I will!" Frida grabbed Dra—'s upper arm. "And I will be as frank with you as I like, do you understand?"

"Yes."

"I don't think you do. Pleasure is unbearable: you'll see how we must endure it. Love weakens pleasure—I heard them saying that, too—in the mailroom." Frida turned again to the wall, and finding a small wen there, dug her fingers into it, grunting.

"Why?" Dra— asked. "Why did they say that?"

"What do you care?" Frida smiled. "Me, I'm almost always alone, thinking about fire and poison and a thousand ways to die. Do you think we're immortal? I don't. But there's a little thrill in believing we are. 'Who cares?' is what I say. I only hope that when I die someone will be sitting next to me, that they won't have gone into the kitchen." Grimly, she kicked one of the doors hard, and it opened.

"Oh, wouldn't a small, neat bathroom be much better than this one?" Frida said, voice disappointed and echoing wildly, for indeed, the room was as large as a gymnasium, misty and bare, with toilets along the far wall in a row so long it faded from sight, and in the corner nearest them sat a small, neat office.

Next to the office was a special type of toilet that appeared to be able to fold out from the wall in any number of configurations so that users might position themselves according to desire. Nearby, a few heavy ropes hung from the ceiling and gently brushed the floor.

"You might think my opinions are troubling and perhaps they are," Frida said, sniffing as they stood in the bathroom's humid, silent vestibule. "But I'm a deep thinker. Are you?"

"I think in my sleep. My thoughts move in order."

"Oh. Well," Frida said with a glance, "I'm older, educated by school, so I am aware of all the awful things there are to be afraid of. The young don't know about these things."

"Some imagine awful things anyway!"

"Naturally they do. Oh," Frida said, looking around, spreading her hands, "isn't the air wonderful to breathe in a quiet room like this? Sometimes it's just good to breathe for a few moments before using the toilet, don't you agree? Did you see anything floating in the bowls?" she added worriedly.

"No."

"Good," was the reply, and together they approached the row of toilets, their footsteps echoing around them, Frida whimpering as Dra— leaned to one of the toilets and delicately opened its enormous lid with her fingertips, a task that drained her so terribly that afterward she sank to the floor to rest.

"I want to see the future," Frida whispered. "I want to know how and when I will die, is that so terrible?"

"I don't want to know," she responded.

"I'll bet you do! Deep down, I'm sure you'd like to know how you'll die. Do you feel like every drop of pleasure you experience brings you closer to death? I do. I'd like to see the world in a thousand years when there's nothing left but rubble and little pieces of plastic everywhere, wouldn't that be the best revenge?"

"Revenge for what?"

Frida only laughed. "Are you an optimist or a pessimist?"

"Well," Dra— said slowly, "I'm nothing, I suppose."

"Yes!" screamed Frida, pulling Dra— to her feet. "Yes! That's just what I am! I'm nothing! Sometimes I wait all day at school to realize that I'm nothing, and that nothing will ever happen to me! Do you? When I imagine all sorts of musty little pathways leading us to a better life, I get a little sick! I hate school! Even when I wear a suit with a sweater underneath I feel unprotected, do you? I'm sick of pretending to have a grand time! I can't remember the first half of my life, but what of it?" Frida hid her face, beginning to cry. "Do you have a charm bracelet?" she asked meekly through her hands.

Dra— answered inaudibly as Frida cried for a while, loudly, as if with relish. Finally, sniffing, Frida asked: "Are you ill?"

"No."

"Yes, you are. Who isn't? You're ill; you're filled with poison; you'll lose your hair and die like everyone else. There's nothing we can do to stop it, short of a long-range revolt against the way things are!"

Dra— answered: "Then you're no different—you'll get sick too!" and Frida knelt and cried weakly against the wall.

They remained silent for long minutes near the toilets, hearing, from far away, a few trepid clicks like the footsteps of someone about to come forth. Frida raised her head and whispered intensely, "If you think your body is conspiring against you, you're probably right, that's what bodies do. And if you assume someone is conspiring against you, they're probably not, but if you ask them about it, they'll trick you by saying they are." She sighed. "An hour before I met you I got a little sick, but no throw-up," she confessed morosely.

Frida blew her nose into a small handkerchief and glanced around the room. "Stay with me while I use the toilet, won't you? I can't wait any more." She looked at Dra—. "Do you have to go too?"

Though admitting so seemed an enormous compromise of integrity, Dra— nodded; and at the sight of Frida tearing down her underwear, she winced, saying, "Yes!" and together the two rushed to the toilets, groaning.

For long minutes they sat, side by side on the row of toilets, heads down, breathing as the light from the room's opaque windows seemed to fade, and a different time of day to ensue. Presently, Dra— looked up to survey Frida's back, entirely bare, for in the frenzy, Frida had torn her uniform away, and also her shoes, so that she now sat stiffly, uncomfortably, lip jutted, uniform bunched in her lap.

"My mother has gone away," she whispered straight ahead of her, "to Hungary, and I'm not sad, I'm not glad, I'm not anything at all. I have no opinion on the subject, in other words, so don't bother asking me about it."

"All right."

"And my clothing will never touch a toilet seat, either, if I have control over anything in this world," Frida continued expressionlessly, then mouthed several words to herself before jumping from the toilet, landing hard on her soles. In a moment she had dressed, and looked at Dra— earnestly.

"Once I finish with the bathroom I don't feel so alone, and it's all over 'til the next time. That's how I live, do you see? It's not so bad, really; some people have worse."

"Some have spells," offered Dra—, but Frida did not seem to hear this.

They flushed their toilets in tandem, staring at the wild motion in the bowls. After a moment Frida gripped Dra—'s arm, pointing to the water, which was rising dangerously close to the tops of the toilets, and began to spill over. "Oh," Frida sobbed, "Dammit! Dammit!" She took up her shoes and barreled through the doorway, wildly upset; and Dra— ran behind her through the sour-smelling hall until they reached an abandoned worksite covered in rubble.

Frida fell against the wall in relief, saying between sharp, heaving breaths, "I just hate when that happens! It's as if the world is coming to an end!" then gradually breathed more slowly, saying she felt much better, and hoped to be married soon.

"Oh," Frida smiled warmly at Dra—, now strangely relaxed. "Shouldn't you think about it as well? I never thought I'd say this, but—elope! We both will! Shouldn't we elope? Yes, it's best. Not for us the nervous preparations. Elope, that's what I'm going to do," she said looking upward and smiling tremblingly. Her hands pressed against the tile wall. "Anything else would be much too inconvenient. Of course we will need blood tests for

diseases. What if it all were to happen so suddenly, say—
tomorrow? We would need the tests today—right now,
in fact. The grooms could be tested later, in their sleep.
What do you think?" Her face was flushed and imploring. "As a student nurse, I can administer the test now, so
we'll be nearer than ever to elopement," Frida concluded
excitedly, turning to run again.

"Blood is always drawn through the right wrist, provided the skin is intact and unremarkable," Frida shouted
over her shoulder, far down the corridor; Dra— followed,
wobbling. Ahead, she saw Frida jamming various keys
into the lock of what appeared to be a small closet, but
which on approaching she saw to be a fully equipped
laboratory, its shelves loaded with suture, gauze, and
other supplies. "I will draw your blood, then my own, as
is the way of the schools," sang Frida as she settled onto a
stool and reached for a set of small hollow needles, which
she began to moisten.

She produced a black cord and wrapped it tightly
around Dra—'s wrist, causing the heel of the hand to
bulge and redden. "Blood is an enormous transporter of
nutrients," Frida said breathlessly, and tied several more
cords in an elaborate fashion along Dra—'s entire arm, at-
taching to each of these an additional, longer cord, which
could be tugged from a distance, it seemed. "I hope you
realize that. We must be vigilant around the blood and
bodies of other people but—how close is too close? is my
question. Why is wanting to sniff the scent of someone
else's blood, or even wanting to swim in it, too close?
Why? I don't understand."

"I don't know either," Dra— answered sullenly, eyes

taking in a shelf stacked with wrapped, sterilized scissors.

"Ah, I think I'm beginning to understand you!" Frida exclaimed, holding the needle ready in front of her.

"This blood —" Dra— began to say, perspiring, pointing to her arm, but she could not finish her thought; and Frida, her curly hair rising with the heat, awkwardly grasped the top of Dra—'s forearm with one hand and pointed the needle in the other.

But Frida used too little force, and the blood did not issue from the vein; she tried a few more times, but without success. Unsustainably tired, slumping, Dra— realized that she was dropping off to sleep, possibly due to the unpleasantness of the blood test.

She awakened not too many minutes later; Frida, still seated next to her, was angling and aiming the needle in the air as if in practice. She looked at Dra—, then quickly brought a moss-colored cloth to the side of her mouth, wiping, remarking, "You have mucho saliva!" Frida's dark eyes were excited as she went on, "Do you think it's better to keep relationships cool and contained, or to let all hell break loose?"

And Dra— said she surely did not know, and then grew sleepy again, perhaps only because of the fearful anticipation that she would, in fact, fall asleep. That would displease Frida, she thought — and at that moment, Frida pricked the needle on her inner wrist, hard, so that a tiny drop of blood emerged, and giving a great cry of delight, Frida wiped the drop onto a white tile.

Gushing with sudden warm emotion for Frida, Dra— raised her head and gave forth a large, awkward smile, asking if it was really true about the moment of death, that it was much easier to endure than all the years of illness and combustion leading up to it; and she also asked if the wish to be holy was out-of-date.

Rubbing her wrist, untying the cords, she then decided to tell Frida about The Man with No Hair—his peculiarly weak, absent quality, the numerous times she had seen him pass in the hallways, and his strange, diminutive shoes. Having said this, still sitting on the stool, she lowered her head to the lab counter as Frida looked on and by degrees felt the pleasure of sleep softly coalesce within her; in a dream, she looked down to see a hole in her hand. She saw ruins of smashed elevators and airplanes, and then the Nurse, distant and statuesque, stepping into a hallway to dispose of a beaker of blood. And in sleep she recalled the dark, humid, desire-making cloakrooms of her school days, the small washstands in the corners reeking with mashes of socks and old cafeteria food and soaked notebooks, and in these cloakrooms, the muffled shouts of grown women who stood there every afternoon for long terrible minutes, perhaps on their coffee breaks, small groups of women silhouetted against the old coat racks, all wailing phantasmagorically, teetering as if standing on a balancing-wire, calling out, "Why do you rule?"—perhaps as a general cry directed to the whole world, but also directed toward someone very much in the particular, someone close at hand who was about to receive her just due for inexcusable ignorance and cruelty.

The women in the closet beat their jaws variously with their knuckles, screaming for the airplanes to stop their terrible roaring; and they cried that they couldn't distinguish the word "kiss" from the word "crumble," nor "stop" from "inculcate," and as Dra— peered through the door, they stamped and gasped how they hated their jobs—though that was the least of it—and how they wanted revenge for their vulnerable, sick bodies, and how their disease paralleled the state of the world, and how, after taking their weekly medicine, they despised filling out the Nausea Questionnaire; and how they wanted more than anything not to be burdened anymore by their illness, and by their lack of control in all situations. They cried about never having gained an edge in the world, and how at every turn, tiny, cruel details worked to prevent this, for example the way they felt compelled to be physically small. And at the cloakroom doorway had stood only Cookie, the pragmatic olive-green-faced school ward, who announced over her clipboard, "If you have twenty-four months or less to live, see me," then complained that the women did not understand limits within relationships: "Just because you hadn't any mothering you think you can climb all over me with your bony hands like I was a hill, imagine it, grown ladies with needs so fierce they'd take the breath out of someone if they could—don't you know what 'respect' means?" and then Cookie had sighed, more than disgusted, purplish lips pressed together, and disappeared far into the cloakroom and out its rear door.

Then in sleep, Dra— heard the sonorous, sweet tones of hollow telephones and saw the faces of employees she had seen so often through the years, all of them surging past her through the halls, their faces so familiar they seemed artificial, even that of the bald chorus teacher from school whom she had hated and who, maybe from ubiquitous fear, sweated so profusely at all times that a slippery puddle was perpetually at his feet. He had died on the indoor bridge that led to the auditorium, after imploring a group of students to follow all commandments and rules, even in the face of despair—for despair was false, he said, a trick that prevented one from being competitive and successful in life.

And in sleep, she heard shuffling footfalls that made her raise her head, half-awake, and see the Administrator, who had returned to the room and was saying so warmly and solicitously, "Hello!" bringing with her a scent of lotion.

"You came back?" Dra— asked hoarsely, inexplicably filled with a gladness so uncomfortable that she threw her face back down to her hands on the lab counter, hiding her eyes.

"Naturally!" the woman said, chewing gum with gusto. "Don't you want to be close?"

"What do you mean?" she answered, nearly sick with apprehension.

"Oh, just that we'll hem and haw and whatnot. Who knows what we will do?" The Administrator smiled and tugged at her skirt, adding cheerfully, "Don't you want to need other people?" as she pulled the gum from her mouth and rolled it into a wad, tossing it across the room.

With her eyes, Dra— followed the gum's long, arched course, while a cool sensation of blustering air seemed to lift her, and she rode it helplessly while hearing the strange sound of friends' voices surrounding her and cooing with compassion; she had never heard anything like this before, she realized, scanning her memory, and so the voices, it seemed, must have come from the future.

But there was no place to hide, she thought, rubbing her head, lowering it; not here, not in any office, nor in her old school that was built directly into the walls quite close to this very spot, the steam-laden school where her thoughts still often wandered, with its famished students, molding elevator shafts, floors the color of spilled bucket-water—and its blankish character, too, which she knew she somehow shared.

No one in the school had spoken to her, though, so she was hidden, in effect, without having to hide. During her time there she made frequent, frustrating solitary visits to the school's bathrooms via echoing, sopping wet hallways, stopping along the way to moan and dig her fingernails deeply into the soft wall-grout, an old habit whose origin she simply did not know.

And against the fixity of her rock-hard stomach, she also recalled a classmate, now dead, who once from in between empty library shelves had poked forth her gullish eyes and shouted to the silent, gaping library class: "I'm married!" then shoved a small metal chest to the floor, scattering wigs and electrical switches everywhere.

She remembered the school's vice-principal, who, after killing a mouse on the lunchroom carpet, had taken her into his office where they sat and stared shyly at one another for many minutes in silence. What was left of his parched-looking hair, badly thinned by disease and medicine, was mostly hidden by a small cotton cap; nevertheless, he was rather vibrant, and not too weak. "I like you," she had said to him in a kind of fomenting exhaustion, puzzled with herself, her eyes fairly burrowing into his jacket front, and they both turned away.

"It is desire that you now feel. By all accounts, the name we give this emotion is desire," he answered softly to the wall, perhaps just as exhausted as she; "You give me evidence enough—look at your hands—but my training tells me that this feeling may actually be the product of rage. Do you understand how rage can mimic other emotions?"

Uncharacteristically, she rose from her chair then and in a scream accused him of unfairness, but he only shook his head and waited with her until she grew quiet again, looking down to regard his own shaking hands and limbs, perhaps the result of decades of working with students. Eventually, all the lights in the school went off, and the cook came to escort them each to midnight meetings.

But now, brushing away these memories, she looked to the Administrator, who waited, eyes shimmering with sympathy, and who, after some time, dusted off her stockings with a palm, saying, "Which do you feel is worse? Tethers, or the boundless opportunity to run free?"

Not answering this, Dra— went on to remark, "But what if it becomes a worse fate to know a person, rather than not to know them—what is there to do then?"

The Administrator stared. "Holler?"

"Oh—!" she cried.

"It's not so unusual to need other people, is it, or even to fear losing them?" the woman said tenderly. "Why, most employees are afraid to lose anything at all, even a nail. And we all know how sad little children feel when they watch their feces flushed down the toilet."

With a vague nod indicating both assent and confusion, Dra— continued, "But what if we find ourselves lying next to another person at night? Shouldn't we keep as still as possible, so as not to annoy them? What if that person tries to hold our hand and discourages us from having private thoughts of our own? Should we comply, just for the sake of lying next to another human being? In those moments, is there really anything left of oneself at all?"

The Administrator sighed as silent tears slid from her eyes and she helped Dra— from the laboratory stool, leading her by the hand across the hallway and into a small auditorium where, at its far end, a white drape stirred. They heard scraping, shearing sounds, perhaps distant electrical saws, as they crossed the floor and the Administrator drew back the drape. There, in another dim room, Dra— saw with surprise the man, the one she had seen so many times before, the one with no hair with whom she so often had wanted to speak—he was lying above them in a hammock-like net suspended from the ceiling by two long black cords. The net rocked slightly with the man's weight, and positioned on his stomach, he lifted his head toward them, smiling tightly with obvious anger.

Wiggling his torso, the man began to swing the net back and forth; and incredulously Dra— turned to the Administrator, who stood behind her, a look of deep concentration in her eyes.

Dra— surveyed the walls of the small room, bare except for a long plastic sack sagging with weight, perhaps feces, hanging upon the wall. The man rose nearer to the ceiling with each swing, growing agitated, squealing, whinnying through a clenched jaw. He arched his neck and head, attempting to buck his legs, though they were tied into the net, it seemed, by a light twine; and rising nearly to the ceiling with each swing, he stretched and contracted his body with great distress, shuddering in sudden anger, face and neck scarlet. Growling, he sailed toward the ceiling as if to catapult himself against it with a force that would smash the crown of his head. Then, he dropped his head back down into the woven surface of the net.

Dra— seized her face in her hands, unable to look; yet as he sailed past once more she caught his sour scent and cautiously, curiously raised her head, uncovering her eyes to stare with disturbed disbelief.

"I suppose it really is rather hard on the neck, in general, to hold up the head," the Administrator was saying.

"It's difficult to believe, but he loves being up there," she went on. "He tied himself in—he won't come down! I've tried lures, I've tried plain talk. But that was a mistake—it only whetted his stubbornness! It keeps me awake at night sometimes, wondering why he won't relent. Well, he craves motion, for one thing."

Swinging above, the man looked down at the Administrator and screamed, "No more secret agreements!"

The Administrator shielded her face. "What do you mean?" she called. "There really are none! Not here, not involving me," but the man responded with a hot, long, angry scream as he swung insensibly to and fro and tears oiled his lean, sallow face.

"Maybe he feels most alive up there," the Administrator said wonderingly. "Yesterday, when I asked him why it gives him such pleasure,"—her voice rose to the man—"he only laughed and said, 'Dogs have their day!'"

A tone sounded, and the Administrator went to the wall shelf, from which she pulled a fine, hairlike telephone made of, it seemed, strands of filament, which she wrapped around her hand before holding the instrument to her ear. The caller must have been very close to her, Dra— reasoned, for the Administrator did not speak, but only made a single, soothing affirmative tone in her throat before putting the phone away.

The Administrator turned back to Dra—. "I've been trying to keep him from being locked away in an awful, awful place! He can't go to work now, you see. But rage is not so odd, after all," she mused, facing Dra— with a look of copious, concerned interest. "Neither is fear."

Again she took Dra—'s hand. "Once, I knew a young man who contained such terrible rage inside him that one night, his pupil blew out. I knew a girl once, too, whose heart spat out all its blood and, breathing only air, it died. I asked myself, 'What if you were in that position, suffering so from rage?' Of course you'd think about your mother, but beyond that I really must admit that I wouldn't know what to do," she gently concluded.

She called out to the man, "Come and be with us? Won't you come down?" as he sailed past again, laughing in an upset manner.

"I hear what you say!" he screamed. "I've heard you at night, too, talking through the intercoms. Oh," he crowed, clenching and unclenching his hands on the sides of the net, "I have known for the longest time that you keep secrets!"

Looking burdened, the Administrator tugged at Dra—'s arm, turning to leave. "There are so many theories, but none is adequate or even true! Perhaps there's nothing we can do for him," she said sadly, while above the man steered and twisted the net in a deft manner such that he skimmed within a few inches of their heads, then rose quickly toward the ceiling.

He began to scream fitfully, face growing purple, and he pumped his body in order to swing the net even higher, nearly upending himself. Sweat dropped sadly from his face and presently the swinging slowed; then he lay limp in the net, face pressed into its ropes. He raised his head. "Don't leave," he called out in a different tone, and he pointed to his wrapped feet, which were very sore, he said, owing to a recent course of surgery.

"Exhaustion prevents me from being more articulate, but let me try," he said. "My former Administrator wanted to talk to me about my feet, but before she could, I opted for surgery instead. The toes needed a considerable thinning; they were far too wide, unreasonably so, and they weren't long enough either, and the spaces between each toe needed to be deepened. So the doctor took care of it. It was a success all around! My ears needed to be clipped and flattened too, a routine piece of work, so he did that as well. But I chose surgery all on my own, with no prompting from anyone! I was proud of that. When my feet and ears heal, the scars will grow into webs of skin that will also need to be cut away, but after that, the entire ordeal will be finished. That excites me!"

He fell back into the net, which rocked imperceptibly above them, and he sang quietly to himself, as if that helped him negotiate his exhaustion.

STACEY LEVINE is the author of *My Horse and Other Stories*, *Dra—*, *Frances Johnson,* and *The Girl with Brown Fur: Tales and Stories.* She has received a PEN/West Award and *The Stranger*'s Genius Award for Literature in 2009. She lives in Seattle, Washington.